# A
# A COUNTRY SONG

*Cowboy Dreamin' 7*

**Sandy Sullivan**

**Erotic Romance**

**Secret Cravings Publishing**
www.secretcravingspublishing.com

**A Secret Cravings Publishing Book**
Erotic Romance

Kiss Me, Cowboy
Copyright © 2015 Sandy Sullivan
Print ISBN: 978-1-63105-507-2

First E-book Publication: January 2015
First Print Publication: January 2015

Cover design by Dawné Dominique
Edited by Stephanie Balistreri
Proofread by Sarah Biggs
All cover art and logo copyright © 2015 by Secret
Cravings Publishing

**PUBLISHER**
Secret Cravings Publishing
www.secretcravingspublishing.com

# Dedication

This book is dedicated to those two special Jackson
fans.
You know who you are.
They have been chomping at the bit for this book, so
here it is.
I hope you enjoy Jackson and Samantha's story.
This one was an emotional piece to write for many
reasons, but alcoholism is a scary and difficult process
for both the addicted person and the family.
If you think you may have an alcohol problem, please
seek help.

Sandy Sullivan

# A COWBOY AND A COUNTRY SONG

## Sandy Sullivan

## Chapter One

Joshua stood at the bottom of the stairs, looking over the group at the table as Jackson continued to eat. "Are you coming, Jackson?"

"Chill. I'm almost done. I'll meet you two outside."

"Fine, but we need to get moving. The concert starts in three hours. It's an hour drive to San Antonio."

Jackson pushed his plate away and stood. "I know how far it is, asswipe. I've lived here as long as you have, plus I've driven there plenty of times. We'll be fine."

"But we have backstage passes to meet her, and Candace wants to get there in plenty of time."

"We have lots of time. Ease up, man."

They were headed to a benefit concert Candace had helped plan for a local children's hospital in San Antonio. He'd volunteered to do security for a country music star during this benefit concert although he wasn't sure why. Yeah, he knew who Samantha Harris was. Even he could admit she was one hot number, but he didn't know about being her bodyguard for the night. Oh well, he didn't have anything better to do. He might as well follow around the leggy blonde and keep the overzealous fans at bay. He couldn't do worse, he figured. At least he'd be where the action was.

Joshua met Candace at the bottom of the stairs with a kiss to her lips.

"Are we ready?"

"Yeah, we are just waiting for Jackson, Mr. Head of Security."

"I'm coming, jeez!" Jackson got up from the table, placed his hat on his head and swept his hand wide, motioning for them to hurry up now.

Joshua and Candace followed him out to the truck. "I'm taking my own," Jackson announced. "I want to have my own vehicle."

"Fine. Do you know how to get there?"

"Of course, I do."

"Great. We'll see you there."

An hour later, they pulled into the Alamodome back parking lot where security was told to park. He and Candace stepped out of their truck with Jackson parked next to them.

"Can I help you?" One of the security personnel standing near two huge semi-tractor trailers with Samantha Harris' picture all over them asked in a clipped tone.

"I'm Candace Alexander, this is my fiancé, Joshua Young, and his brother, Jackson Young."

"Ah, yes. Ms. Harris told me you would be arriving soon. The command post for security has been set up to the left. Ms. Harris is on her bus near the back there. She said to send you right over, Ms. Alexander."

"Thank you. Jackson, I guess you need to check in with security so they can tell you where you need to be. I told them you were to be near Samantha at all times."

"Right." He saluted smartly before wandering over to the tent with his hands in his pockets. As he walked near, the other guys all stood around with radio pieces in their ear talking to each other. "I'm Jackson Young. I'm supposed to report to you guys?"

"Hi. I'm Trevor. I'm head of security for Ms. Harris. You'll be guarding her one on one throughout the night according to Ms. Alexander. Since you're dressed like everyone else here, you should blend in well. I will give you an earpiece though, so we can talk, and you can let me know if there are any issues. Sound good?"

"Yep." Trevor handed him an earpiece and a transmitter for his back pocket. After he placed the piece in his ear, he tested the microphone clipped to his shirt. Trevor gave him the thumbs up.

"You are to be with her at all times. Right now, she's in her bus so just hang out around the door until she needs you to escort her to the backstage area. She'll be doing meet and greets after the show in the back. Keep her secure at all times."

"Got it." He wandered back toward the big brown bus with a huge scrolling SH on the side. Her personal bus. *Hmm*. He wondered what it was like on the inside. Pretty fancy, he imagined. She didn't seem to be the type of girl who went without her comforts of home as much as she was on the road. Not that he paid a lot of attention to her tour schedule or anything, but he knew where she'd be the next six weeks. Okay, yeah, he had a bit of a fascination with Samantha Harris. Who wouldn't? She was a pretty hot woman. He definitely wouldn't mind being her personal roadie for a few nights.

The door flew open on the bus. Joshua, Candace and Samantha came down the stairs. In a heartbeat Samantha bolted around them to head to the back. "Who the hell are you and what are you doing loitering around my bus? Speak up, cowboy, I don't have all day!"

Samantha got right up in his face, giving him his first up close and personal look at the leggy blonde. She wasn't wearing her customary black Stetson. The black short-sleeved blouse emphasized her gorgeous breasts for his enjoyment. The jeans she wore hugged her hips, showing off her legs to perfection. Long blonde hair hung to the middle of her back in a long, straight braid. He wanted to undo it so he could run his fingers through the soft strands. What drew him the most were her eyes. The blue orbs spit fire, right at that moment. "Ma'am?"

"Don't ma'am me, mister. If you don't have any business being back here, get lost."

"I'm Jackson, ma'am."

"Jackson?"

Candace introduced him, indicating he had reason to be there. "Samantha Harris, meet Jackson Young, your security detail. He is Joshua's older brother."

"Security detail?"

"Yeah, Sam. Jackson is your personal bodyguard for the night."

"Well, shit on a stick. Sorry. I didn't mean to go off on you so hard, but I'm always finding people hanging around my bus who shouldn't be."

"That's what I'm here for, ma'am. There won't be any loitering tonight. Unless they have a pass, they won't be allowed near you, and if you give me the nod to get rid of them, I'll handle it."

Sam gave him a saucy wink. "Good. I need a decent man to guard my ass."

"I'd be right honored to guard it for you, ma'am."

Samantha's eyebrow shot up as she smiled, planting her hands on her hips. "I like you. We'll get along just fine." She swung around to face Candace and Joshua. "What do you want to do? Have you two eaten?"

"Yeah. We ate before we came."

"We could get some good alcohol so we can party on my bus before the concert. I don't go on for a while."

"Sound good to me," Candace replied. "I haven't had a good drunk on in some time." She wrapped her arm around Joshua's waist. "Since I have my personal guy here, I can get drunk if I want. He can carry me home."

"Anytime, babe."

Candace stood on her tiptoes to kiss him on the lips. "I love you."

"I love you too."

"You two are too cute. Someday, I'll have that, but for now I sing."

"You're good at it too."

"Thanks, doll." Samantha glanced his direction, giving him the once over from the top of his hat to the tips of his boots. He wondered if she liked what she saw. "You might as well come too, cowboy, if you are to be my bodyguard. I never know when someone will get a little too crazy."

"My pleasure, ma'am."

"And quit calling me ma'am. I feel like I'm forty or something."

"You can't be over twenty-five."

She tossed back her head on her shoulders and laughed, a full gut rolling, belly laugh that sounded full. "I love you already!" She linked her arm with his, leading their group through the maze of buses, big rigs, and people, giving them the complete tour as they walked. Her descriptions of everything that went on in putting together a tour the size of hers, baffled him. "I have over a one hundred people at each stop putting together the stages, getting the lights set up, putting together the sound equipment, and handling the details. It's a major production."

He liked having her on his arm. He didn't like the looks he was getting from the other people in the security detail. It wasn't his fault she'd taken a liking to him, right?

"How long have you been in this business, Samantha?" Joshua asked.

"Ten years, give or take. I've been headlining my own shows for about five years now. Let me tell you, they are a pain in the ass to do. If I would have really understood all the work involved in being the headliner, I would have stayed as an opener for someone else and let them worry about all the crap."

"You are a very popular country music artist though. Wouldn't that seem weird?" Candace's voice got a little louder as some of the bands who would be opening for Samantha started their sound checks.

"Yeah, I guess so. I was kind of pushed into doing it when I got a little more popular than the closing artist. Hitting several number ones in a row helped."

"I can imagine."

"Do you listen to country music, Jackson?"

"Yes."

"Who is your favorite artist?"

"You."

She laughed. "You're saying that because you are guarding me tonight, but I love you for it anyway."

Little did she realize, he was telling the truth. She was one of his favorite artists in country music these days, but she didn't need to know that right now. He didn't want her to get all weirded out by his little infatuation with her. She might think he was some kind of a stalker or something.

At one point they sat in the stands and listened to the other bands warm up. Most of them were pretty good, but he knew Samantha would blow them out of the water, she was that good.

They continued on their little tour, finally ending up back at her bus about an hour later.

"I need to start getting ready." She tipped her head toward Candace. "You guys have front row seats. Talk to the guy at the ticket booth. They are in there for you under your name."

"Thanks, Samantha." Candace rocked back on her booted heels.

Joshua still hadn't been able to get the girl into a regular pair of cowboy boots. She still wore her high heeled, pointed toe boots. Jackson grinned to himself. He really liked Candace. She was the perfect girl for his brother.

When Samantha spoke again, his attention zeroed in on her lips.

"You're welcome. I figured it's the least I can do since you went to all the work to put this thing together for the children's hospital." She glanced his way. "If you would just guard the bus while I'm inside, that would be great."

"My pleasure."

A pretty smile lifted the corners of her mouth and he had the insane urge to lean in and press his lips to hers. *Yeah, not a good idea.* Her gorgeous eyes sparkled with pleasure as she studied his face.

Candace and Joshua waved to him as they walked back toward the barricade between the fans and her bus. There was already a crowd gathering, waving signs, shouting, and making a general ruckus.

"Samantha, baby, I love you!" a tall guy in a black hat hollered.

Samantha laughed as she waved to the guy. "Don't worry about them unless one breaks through the barricade."

"Gotcha."

"Thanks." She waited for a minute or so before she smiled again and disappeared inside her bus, closing the door tightly behind her.

"Hey, dude!"

Jackson turned toward the guy who shouted over the noise of the crowd. He hesitated before he took several steps in the guy's direction.

"What?"

"Are you like her personal bodyguard?"

"Yeah."

"I just want to talk to her. Can you get me in?"

"Nope."

"Come on, man. A hundred bucks. Right here. In my hand." The guy flashed a hundred dollar bill. "I would love to get close to her. I think she would totally dig me, man. If I could just fuck her one time, I'd be in total heaven. I wouldn't hurt her or nothing. I mean I would totally bang her into tomorrow."

Jackson didn't even hesitate. He wanted to deck the guy for even thinking about Samantha, much less trying to bribe him to let the dude get near her. Wasn't happening. Not today, not ever. Jackson signaled for one of his fellow security people. When the guy got close, he tipped his head. "The guy in the black Stetson needs to go. He's talking about getting too close to Miss Harris."

"I'll take care of it." The burly guy stepped up to the man, talking in low tones. When the guy took a swing at the security detail, three more guys jumped on him.

Jackson smiled as he went back to his post standing guard at her door. His own thoughts went haywire as his imagination drifted to what she might be doing in there, as she got ready for her concert. Changing clothes? Doing her hair? Her makeup? She looked fabulous when he'd seen her before, so he couldn't think of what she needed to do to get ready.

He hoped she left her long blonde hair hanging loose. He loved her hair down and straight although she tended to curl it for shows, from what he'd noticed as he'd followed her career. She usually sported a black cowboy hat, jeans, boots, and a pretty, fitted blouse. Damn, she always looked good enough to eat.

The vision of her standing naked in front of him flashed before his eyes. He cleared his throat as he turned so he wasn't facing the crowd behind the barricade. The last thing he needed was for them to see his hard-on. After several deep breaths and thoughts about branding a calf including the wrestle, the sights, the smell, and the possibility of getting kicked in the junk, he managed to calm his erection to a manageable level.

He heard the crowd before he saw them swarm the seating area. *Wow*. Thousands of people pushed each

other as they scrambled for the best seats in the front
area of the opening seating. Thank God, Joshua and
Candace had reserved seats so they didn't have to fight
the crowd.

Once everyone got inside, the DJ from the local
radio station roused them up again.

"How is everyone tonight?"

The crowd erupted.

"What a group. Are you all ready for some rowdy
country music?"

The crowd went wild with cheers.

"We are here tonight to welcome you all to the
rowdiest country music festival to grace San Antonio in
a decade, but let's not forget the real reason we are here
tonight, folks. This is a benefit show put on by some of
country's *hottest* acts for the benefit of San Antonio's
premiere children's hospital. We are raising money for
families who might be facing medical bills they can't
pay. There are barrels all over the grounds for you to
donate in. Please be generous for the kids. Now, it is
my great pleasure to introduce you to one of the best
upcoming acts in the business today."

For the next two hours, he heard some great music
while he stood guarding Samantha's door. Not once did
she pop her head out during that time and he had to
wonder what the hell she was doing in there by herself.

* * * *

Samantha Harris watched the crowd from behind
the curtain on her bus as her stomach knotted into a ball
of nerves. She loved singing, but she never thought of
herself as good enough for all the hype everyone said
about her. Not like she was Carrie Underwood or

someone like her. That girl had talent. She was only a small town girl from Iowa who liked to sing in the church choir and happened to be discovered one night singing karaoke at a local country bar a few years ago.

She blew out a nervous breath before taking a sip of the whiskey in her hand. The alcohol helped, it always eased the nerves before a show. She just had to be careful not to indulge too much or she would mess up on stage. She glanced at the bottle sitting on the counter. *Half a bottle wasn't too much, right?*

Things seemed to be going well lately, multi-million dollar recording contract, busy multi-venue tour, and screaming fans by the thousands. Why did she feel like shit all the time? Why the nerves?

What about finding the man of her dreams?

This life didn't lend well to finding someone who wasn't after her money or her fame. She knew that already. It had happened twice so far and she didn't think she could go through it again. Was it so hard to find someone nice who wasn't trying to further his own career by hooking up and riding piggyback on hers? All she wanted was a nice cowboy who didn't see her as Samantha Harris the country music star, but Samantha Harris the girl from Iowa.

She smiled as the first band came out blazing. They were good, although they hadn't been around long. She liked them a lot. Their music was great, their lead singer had talent and they had a fantastic sound. They would go far in this business.

Her cell phone jingled a familiar tune from its spot on the table across from her. "Hey Daddy."

"Hey, baby girl."

"What's up? There isn't anything wrong, is there?"

"No, honey. Everything is fine. Your mama and I are doing well. I just knew you were doing a big benefit concert tonight, and I wanted to wish you luck. Are you doing all right?"

"Yeah, just nervous."

"There is no reason for you to be nervous, baby. You are one hell of a singer."

"Thanks, Dad."

"Are you being careful? There are some real crazy nut jobs out there who would love to get close to you."

"I'm careful. I have a great security team. I even have my own personal bodyguard this time. He's the brother of the coordinator. Real cowboy from what I can tell."

"You know what they say."

She laughed. "No, what?"

"A real cowboy can protect what's his with one shot, a well-placed fist, or a bunch of friends."

A giggle burst from her lips. "I love you, Dad."

"I love you too, honey. Break a leg and I don't mean literally. Tell that cowboy your dad said to watch out for you with an eagle eye, and I'll pay him double what you are paying him."

"Stop it, now. I'm sure he can take good care of me without your extra incentive."

"I love you, baby. Be safe and we'll talk to you later this week."

"Bye, Daddy."

She hung up the phone with a little tear in her eye. She missed her parents, missed the farm they owned, missed the horses, donkeys, cows, chickens, and all the other animals she grew up with. Now she never had time for anything for herself. It was always work, always recording, writing new songs, listening to new material, doing publicity shots, more and more, and more. Some days she wanted to quit, go back to her life in Iowa to forget this craziness had ever been, but she couldn't. The multi-record deal with her record company said so. They called the shots as much as she hated to admit it.

"Sam. You're on in thirty minutes."

"Thanks, Darryl," she called. She quickly downed the remainder of the whiskey in her glass before refilling it with three fingers more worth of the brown, potent liquid.

She glanced out the window. The cowboy paced back and forth in front of her door. Jackson Young. She had to think about it a minute before she could remember, not that she didn't think he was hotter than a firecracker on the Fourth of July, but the whiskey had blurred her memory a bit. She really should quit before the show. No matter. The guys in the band would take care of her, they always did.

When he moved back in front of the door, she could see the breadth of his shoulders stretched the nice shirt he wore. The hat on his head wasn't a cheap one either. *I wonder what he normally does for a living. Surely he doesn't do private security all the time. He looks like a real-deal cowboy from the top of his head to the boots on his feet.* "Hmm." She brought the glass to her lips, but didn't sip. The vapor from the whiskey burned her nose a little, forcing her to set the glass back on the table next to her. Thoughts about Jackson floated through her mind as she wondered more about him. Does he ride? Is he good with animals? Maybe he does rodeo. She kind of liked men who rode horses, roped, busted broncs, did normal cowboy stuff. After all, she was a cowgirl herself from way back, born and bred by a father who had the belt buckle of a champion calf-roper himself.

Jackson's hair brushed the collar of his shirt, making her fingers tingle to feel if the strands were as soft as they looked. He had his arms crossed over his chest as he stood guard over the door to her bus. She felt silly having someone specifically there to watch over her, but it was needed since she had a stalker these days. They didn't know who he was, only that he sent messages to her through security or someone else close to her. It was kind of scary to think the person could get that close.

Jackson knocked on the door. "Are you ready, Ms. Harris?"

She blew out a breath, downed the rest of the whiskey in her glass, and then stood. Her head swam a bit, but she was used to that. The alcohol would calm her enough she could perform without being terrified of singing in front of thousands of people. She'd become a pretty good actress when it came to acting sober. She checked her appearance in the mirror over the sink. Curls, check. Lipstick, check, black cowboy hat…she grabbed it from the sofa. Check. She was as ready as she'd ever be.

The knock sounded again. "I'm coming."

When she pushed open the door, Jackson held out his hand to help her down from the high step of the bus. Her boot heel hooked on the bottom step as she pitched forward right into his arms.

"Whoa there."

She glanced up into his face, drowning in the grey of his eyes. Her lips parted as she sighed.

"Are you all right?"

"Uh, yeah. Fine."

His brow furrowed as he frowned while he helped her back onto her feet. She stepped out of his arms reluctantly. She liked being in his arms. They made her feel safe, unlike anyone else she'd ever been near. *That's odd. I don't even know this guy.*

"Why don't you take my arm and I'll escort you to the stage. You're on in fifteen minutes."

"That would be great. I hope I'm not coming down with something. I feel kind of woozy." She put her hand to her head. "I took some cold medicine before I came out here."

"Are you sick?"

"I think so. My nose has been stuffy all day. I think I'm coming down with a cold. I hope my voice holds up. Viruses can be hell on a singer."

He looped her hand through the crook in his arm to escort her toward the stairs leading up to the stage. The third of the opening bands had almost finished their set so she would be up next. "I can imagine."

The crowd went wild as the last band finished their set. They had to know her set came next.

"Thank you all for coming tonight," the DJ said as the band took their leave. "We want to tell you all how much we appreciate the donations you are leaving in the barrels for the kids. This means the world to all of us involved in this. Right now I want to introduce our headliner for this evening's festivities."

The crowd screamed as Jackson escorted her up the stairs to just behind the black curtain. She lowered her head to pray for strength, guidance and a whole lot of love from God. She would need it to get through the next ninety minutes of songs.

"Samantha Harris is a five time CMA winner in several categories. She's had eight number one hit records in the last five years. She is a multi-platinum recording artist and this year is up for Entertainer of the Year for the second year running, winning it last year over some of countries hottest superstars. Please help me make welcome our very own, Samantha Harris."

"Go get 'em, tiger."

She glanced at the man next to her with a small smile on her mouth. She really did like him even though she didn't know him very well. "Thanks." She leaned in, kissed him on the cheek before stepping out to greet the crowd.

# Chapter Two

Jackson stood behind the curtain as he listened to Samantha do number after number. She really could sing. She hit every note perfectly in pitch and tone. The voice of an angel, some said. Right now, he could believe it.

He closed his eyes as he let the song drift through him. It was one of his favorites on her current album. He could almost believe she did it just for him.

"How ya'll doing tonight?"

The crowd erupted in shouts.

"I hope you are being generous with your dollars for the kids and their families. This concert is for them." She walked to the edge of the stage. "I have to thank my good friend, Candace Alexander for settin' this up. She's down front here with her fiancé, Joshua. Don't they make a cute couple?"

The television camera broadcasting to the big screen, panned down to where Joshua and Candace stood. Jackson could almost see the blush on Candace's cheeks from the attention. She was a computer geek from way back. He could tell she didn't like the hubbub of the camera on her face.

"I think they should get married up here on the stage. What do you think?"

The crowd shouted their approval as Candace and Joshua shook their heads no.

"Ah, come on you two. You're in love, right?"

Jackson could see Candace's face pale as she turned to face Joshua, shaking her head.

"Oh, you two are no fun. Fine then, how about if I get married tonight?"

The crowd fell silent.

"No really. There is this really cute cowboy who is my security detail. He's Joshua's brother. His name is Jackson. Come on out here, Jackson. I want everyone to see you."

He held back by the curtain. *What the hell is she up to?*

"Hey, camera dude and lighting dude, follow me." She headed toward where he stood.

As the bright white light followed her across the stage, his stomach clenched. He wasn't the type to like the limelight and here she was, bringing it to him.

She held out her hand. "Come here."

Not knowing what else to do, he took her hand in his grasp so she could pull him into the bright lighting.

"Isn't he gorgeous?"

The women erupted into wolf whistles and shouts of encouragement. "Now if there were a preacher around, I'd have him marry us."

"Ms. Harris, this isn't funny."

"I'm serious."

"You don't even know me."

"But I like you." She leaned in. "I think you are cute and I could sure use some time ridin' those hips."

"Why don't you sing some more."

She sighed as she brought herself flush against him, turned her head to the audience and said, "Excuse me a minute."

When she lowered the microphone, he wasn't sure what to expect, but her grabbing the back of his head and slamming her mouth down on his, wasn't it.

This certainly wasn't the way he wanted their first kiss to be.

The feel of her mouth against his threw his heart rate through the ceiling, his libido straight out the end of his dick.

Shouts and catcalls finally brought his brain back to the present as he slowly peeled her off his chest.

"We'll continue this later, cowboy." She stepped back, brought the microphone to her mouth, and began the full out rendition of her current single as she left him in the shadows when the spotlight moved with her across the stage.

He wasn't sure whether to shout out loud because she'd kiss him, turn her over his knee for teasing him like that, or slink back into the shadows as she totally forgot about him in the next second.

For now he would blend back into the backdrop to watch her. The taste of her on his mouth made him frown. If he wasn't mistaken, there was alcohol on her breath, not just from cold medicine either. She hadn't sounded stuffed up earlier when they'd been walking around. He hoped his thoughts were wrong, but he had a feeling they weren't.

He glanced at his watch. She still had several more songs to do before she finished.

With a quick look toward the stage, he turned on his heels to head down the steps. The security detail was otherwise occupied, so he opened the door to her bus and walked up the small set of stairs.

The bus's interior stretched out before him. Its gold and white décor reflected Samantha's style. A smooth leather couch lined one wall with a small table to the left. Opposite them sat a white bench seat. The closed door beyond the kitchen had to be her bedroom. His gaze fell upon the dove guitar in a stand near the kitchenette. She didn't use the beautiful instrument onstage, but he knew she wrote a lot of her own music.

Lavender invaded his nose as he walked slowly toward her door. He wanted to see her personal space, but it wasn't his place. He searched from left to right before he found what he was looking for. A three quarter empty bottle of whiskey, Jack Daniel's to be exact. *I knew it!*

He'd been through hell with Jacob a few times to see the signs. She had an alcohol problem.

"Thank you everyone. You are the best. See you on the road!"

*Shit.*

He scrambled outside, slamming the door before running for the stage to meet her. He managed to skid to a stop at the bottom of the small set of stairs just as she reached the top. Holding his hand out, he helped her down the metal plates until she reached the bottom.

Sweat poured from her temples when she removed her hat. "Wow. What a crowd."

"You did great."

"Thanks."

She wobbled a little as she headed toward her bus while the crowd behind them filed out. Several people had already found their way to the security barricade near her bus. They shouted as they waited for her, hoping she would stop near them, take a few pictures and sign some autographs.

"Man, I need a shower."

"Are you going to greet your fans?"

"Yeah, I need to."

"Are you up to it?"

"It's part of the process, so yeah."

He walked her to the steel gates keeping her fans from trampling her. For the next hour, she greeted fans, signed autographs, took pictures, gave kisses to a few rowdy men although never on the mouth, and did her best to be the star she was.

"I'm done. Let's go."

"That's it folks. Thanks for coming, but Ms. Harris is done for tonight," Jackson said, taking her hand in his to lead her back to her bus.

"I'm beat."

"I bet." He opened the bus door for her, watching as she put her foot on the first step before she glanced back at him.

"Would you join me for a bit? I'd like to talk to you about something."

"Uh, sure, but aren't you afraid of what your fans will think?"

"I guess. Wait a few minutes then and come on in after the majority of them have left. You probably want to say something to your brother and Candace before they leave."

"Yeah."

"Did you bring your own vehicle?"

"Yes."

"Good." She smiled sadly as she pulled the door to the bus closed behind her.

He turned toward the crowd by the gates, noticing Joshua and Candace standing off to the side. When he got to where they stood, he escorted them around the steel barricade and back toward the vehicles sitting toward the rear.

"What the hell was that all about up there?" Joshua asked. "I could have done without the whole 'let's get married' thing."

"Me too." Candace wrapped her arm around Joshua's waist. "I don't know what she was thinking."

"Fuck if I know." He glanced sideways at Candace. "How much do you know about Samantha Harris?"

"Not a lot, why? I mean she's a friend, I guess, but I haven't been around her very much. Mostly just what I know about her is from media."

"I think she might have a drinking problem. She was pretty drunk on stage."

"Drunk?"

"Yeah. I found a three quarter empty bottle of Jack on her table. She tried to pass it off as cold medicine on her breath."

"Wow." Candace bit her lip before saying, "Are you sure?"

"I dealt with Jacob enough on his binges to know someone with an alcohol problem. I seriously think she does. I'm not sure why though. She's talented as all get out."

"Yeah, Jacob was a mess before he got sober."

"She wants to talk to me after the majority of the fans have left." He looked behind Joshua. "Looks like that's now."

Joshua nodded toward the way out. "We're headed home. You be careful."

"I will. I want to talk to her to see if I can find out what's up. Why the drinking before shows. I mean, I know the pressure is hell on performers, but she shouldn't have to drink to the point of getting drunk." With his hands in his pockets, he rocked back on his boot heels.

"Take it easy on her, buddy. She's a pretty nice girl. I don't think she's going to take you butting into her life very easily," Joshua replied.

"I will. I'm not all about getting up in her business. It's not my place, but if she wants to talk, I'll listen."

"We'll catch you later then."

"Be careful going home."

"We will."

He watched as Joshua and Candace headed back for the barricade. Joshua nodded to the security guy when they moved past. The few fans still standing at the gates didn't even seem to notice. They continued to wave signs as they called Samantha's name.

A deep sigh escaped his lips. He wasn't sure how this night might end, but in bed with Samantha wasn't a bad thought. *Jerk. She doesn't need a romping night of sex right now. She needs sympathy, understanding, and a man who will listen.* "Yeah, I can be that for her for the night."

His steps took him back to the bus doors a moment later. A soft knock was answered by a quick come in. He opened the door before taking the first step into her bus, softly closing the door behind him.

"Hi."

"Hey."

He noticed a glass of what looked like soda on the table next to her.

"Can I get you something to drink?"

"What are you having?"

"Coke."

"Sounds good."

She got to her feet before heading to the small kitchen area and the refrigerator. He looked down to realize she was barefoot. Red glossy nail polish graced her toenails. He had to smile. The girlieness seemed completely natural for her. When she bent over to retrieve the can from the shelf, he got a nice view of her round ass in her jeans. He had to admit, she had curves in all the right places.

When she returned to his side, she handed him the soda can before returning to her spot on the opposite side of the coach. Her posture looked relaxed. "I hope security wasn't a big deal for you tonight."

"Nope. Not a problem."

"Good."

"Your performance sounded fantastic."

"Thanks. I always get really nervous before I perform."

"Why? You seem like a natural."

She set her glass of soda on the table before grabbing her hair and pulling it over her shoulder. "I don't know how much you know about me or how I came to be singing for a living, but several years ago if someone told me I'd be standing in front of thousands of people, I would have told them they were crazy."

He took a sip of his Coke. "I'm not sure I understand."

"I got discovered doing karaoke in a bar."

"Wow."

"Yeah. My whole life changed inside of about a week. The record producer offered me a contract and *bam!* The next thing I knew, I was in Nashville, recording a CD, had an agent, and a booking company, fans screaming when they saw me on the street, and the hate of every other country music artist out there because I didn't pay my dues. I never wanted to be a superstar."

"Then why did you allow it to happen? You could have told the producer no."

"I know. Many times I wish I had." She glanced at the Jack Daniel's bottle sitting on the counter. "You know I didn't have cold medicine before the show."

"Yeah, I know."

"I'm sorry I lied to you."

"Don't let it happen again."

She grinned, shook her head and glanced down to where her hands lay in her lap. "You are a hardass, aren't you?"

"Not really. I just know what it's like. I have a sibling who had a drinking problem, so I've dealt with it before."

She jumped to her feet, more pissed off that a wet cat. "I don't have a drinking problem. I have a little alcohol before I go on stage to calm my nerves, but I do *not* have an alcohol problem. I can handle the booze I drink. I mean did I once appear drunk to you?"

"A little."

"I wasn't drunk."

"What was with all the getting married stuff?"

"I thought it would be funny." She spun around to pace from the front to the back of the bus. "Are you saying you wouldn't marry me, given the chance?"

"I don't know you, Ms. Harris."

She stopped her journey when she stood in front of him. "Quit calling me Ms. Harris. That's my mother. I'm Samantha or Sam if you prefer."

"All right, Samantha. No, I wouldn't marry you right now if you wanted me to. I don't take those kinds of things lightly. I don't even know why you would ask since we just met three hours ago."

Deflated, she plopped back down on the couch. "I'm scared, Jackson."

"Scared of what?"

"This whole life, but especially of this person who is stalking me. They have photos of me near my parent's house, on my bus, at truck stops, and the most terrifying thing of all, they know I don't have a steady guy in my life. I don't know if it's a woman or a man, but whoever it is knows way too much about me. I thought if I had a man, they would leave me alone." She shrugged before taking a drink of her soda. "You are as good a choice as any."

"Thanks, I think."

"I didn't mean it as an insult. I'm trying to think of what I can do to discourage this weirdo."

He scraped his hand over the beard covering his face. He liked having whiskers along the bottom of his cheeks, and a mustache framing his mouth meeting with the whiskers along his chin. Women seemed to like how it felt on their skin. The extra scruff also made him stand out a little amongst his brothers who were all clean-shaven. "No insult taken. I'm just trying to figure out where I would fit into the scheme of things."

She bit her lower lip, pulling the plumpness in between her teeth as she concentrated a minute.

He wanted to take it between his teeth and drag it into his mouth to see what she tasted like.

"Maybe we could pretend to be a couple."

"Pretend?"

"Well, that's kind of up to you. I wouldn't mind spending some time with you. You're a gorgeous guy, nice, a cowboy, and you seem to have a good head on your shoulders, but I wouldn't be up for any kind of relationship until we got to know each other. We could pretend to be getting married or something. No one would be able to know about it being fake though. Just you and me."

"What about parents, siblings, etc? Joshua and Candace wouldn't buy this and neither would the rest of my family. They know me better than that."

"I'm afraid they would let the information we weren't really a couple slip."

He looked across the expanse of the bus to where she fiddled with her Coke. "You know you've totally changed the subject."

"Changed the subject from what?"

"Your drinking."

"I already told you, it's not an issue, but this stalker thing is."

He wasn't sure what to do. True, he liked her a lot, but pretending to get married? Nope. Being a couple might have possibilities. He wondered what her plan was. "So, how would this work? I mean your band and everyone here tonight knows I only arrived this evening. They aren't going to buy this either."

"I'll just tell them you've been away on business and arrived only tonight to meet with me. You can go on tour with me. Stay in my bus."

"Wait a minute. We aren't sleeping together are we?"

"Not in the biblical sense of the word, Jackson. I don't know you well enough to spread my legs for you, but there are bunks in this bus behind the door." She pointed to the door closed at the end of the hall. "Down farther is my bedroom which is closed off from the other bunks."

"You want me to move in with you while you are on tour?"

"Yes."

"What about my life on my parent's ranch? I do have a life, you know, outside of obsessing about you, that is."

"You obsess about me?" She grinned as one eyebrow arched over her right eye. "Really?"

"I'm kidding. But I do have a life I can't just walk away from." He thought to himself what exactly his life consisted of on the ranch. Day in and day out, he spent his time doing chores, wrangling cattle, mowing yard, cleaning the pool, taking guests out riding...what else? *Hmm.* It didn't seem so important when you broke things down. "What would your parents say?"

She tucked her feet under her, getting comfortable in the seat like she wasn't going anywhere for a while. Really, where did she have to go? Her next gig?

"Mine are very open-minded. I've already told them you were my security detail, so if you were going to accompany me to protect me, they would be totally cool with the whole thing." She absently braided, then unbraided her hair while she watched him for a reaction, he guessed. The entire process looked like a preoccupied thing she did without realizing she was doing it.

This whole situation sounded crazy. He didn't mind crazy though. It sounded kind of fun and something different than his boring life at Thunder Ridge with all of his siblings pairing off. As one of the remaining single men on the place, he was bombarded with female attention on a daily basis. He didn't mind really, but it got old fending off advances at every turn.

"Mine might be a little weirded out by the situation, but my mom would think it was funny me being tied up with a woman for a couple of months."

He tipped his head to the side. "Just how long are we talking about?"

"I don't know. It depends on how long it takes to flush out the weirdo stalking me. You would be my personal bodyguard the whole time. We would be almost inseparable, you know?"

"Sounds like it."

"What do you say, Jackson? Are you game for a little adventure?"

# Chapter Three

The next thing he knew, they were bumping along the road from the gates of Thunder Ridge with her bus following behind his truck. Samantha sat in the passenger seat holding onto the oh-shit handle, rocking along with the bumps. He told her they could park her bus behind the main lodge until they could find somewhere in town to park it, not that Bandera had a lot of places to hide a forty-five foot long bus. Good thing Thunder Ridge spanned several thousand acres.

He'd called his mom before they headed out toward the ranch to tell her what was going on or at least to let her know he had Samantha Harris in his truck with her bus traveling behind him. Samantha told him she didn't have anywhere to be for a couple of weeks, so they could spend time building their ruse before they took it on the road. He didn't mind getting to know her a bit before this whole thing started.

His mom booked Samantha a room and said to park the bus around back. He'd already given directions to the driver before they left the concert area. They would keep her privacy as much as possible, but they already had several guests at the ranch for the next week. He would do the best he could to protect her from overzealous guests, but he did have his own chores to do.

They pulled up in front of the block wall keeping the parking lot separate from the grass and walkways to the main lodge.

"Wow. What a great place."

"Thanks."

"I love the big house. It's perfect."

"It's the main lodge where meals are taken. We have a pool table, big fireplace, leather couches to just chill out or whatever. The front porch goes all the way along the side of the house. It has several rocking chairs and old antique things sitting out there, where you can relax, watch the sunsets, feed the donkeys…you know, that kind of stuff."

"You have donkeys?"

"Yeah, three to be exact. They are the biggest babies on the ranch. They wander around all the time, bugging the guests for treats or pats."

"I love animals."

"Where did you grow up?"

"Iowa. My parents own a few hundred acres where they breed horses, run a few cattle, and grow corn."

"Doesn't everyone grow corn in Iowa?" He smiled as he shut the truck off.

"Pretty much." She glanced out the windshield, her expression curious as she took it all in. "So this is where you grew up?"

"Yeah. My parents moved here when my oldest brother was still young and I was a baby. They've been running it ever since."

"And you have eight brothers. Wow. I really need to meet your mother."

"You will. She's the glue holding this place together."

"I can imagine. What I can't imagine is raising nine boys."

"Three of those are triplets."

"Holy shit." She turned to face him on the seat. "Are they identical?"

"Yeah. Some people can tell them apart, but others who don't know them very well, can't. You met Joshua. He's one of the triplets along with Joel and Jason."

"Your parents named you all with J names? I bet that's confusing at times."

"Not for us, but yeah, I imagine it gets a little weird. Mom wanted us all named similar to my father. His name is James." He pushed open the door to the truck. "Come on. I'll introduce you to whoever is around."

He met her around the front of the truck, taking her hand in his to lead her up the walkway. Darkness surrounded them even though white solar lights lined the concrete path, brightening the way to the house. Shadows stretched across the yard as clouds moved over the moon in strange patterns. He loved nights like this. October was one of his favorite months of the year even though the weather didn't really turn cooler until later. The evenings tended to drop in temperature as the year wound down toward Christmas. The fall weather always made him think of home and family for some reason.

"Does all of the family live on the ranch?"

"Yeah, but some of my brothers who have paired off have their own places around the property. My parents gifted us all a chunk of land when we turned eighteen. Some of them have built their homes on their piece."

"Where do you live?"

"In the small cabin over there. I shared half of it with Jeremiah until he and Callie got together. They live in town with her father at the moment, until they can get their house built. They just got married a few weeks ago and are on their honeymoon right now."

"How cool."

"Yeah, they got married in Hawaii. Most of us went and stayed for a week or so. It's pretty cool over there. Have you been there?"

"That's one place I haven't been, I think. These tours have me going just about everywhere, including Europe."

"Europe would be fun. I've never been there. I sure would like to see England, Ireland, and a few other countries."

"Maybe I'll take you there someday."

He grinned, but realized this new relationship, if you could call it that, wouldn't be lasting long enough for her to take him anywhere outside of a few states in the U.S. while she did shows. He imagined her schedule was pretty hectic with one show after the other.

They reached the side door of the main lodge, taking the steps quickly. The heavy wood door pushed open with ease as he laid his palm on the panel. Bright lights illuminated the space where they all took meals, almost blinding him as his eyes adjusted. He didn't normally take notice of the things surrounding the room because he went there all the time, but for a moment he took in the western décor. The scorched brand of their place on the walls, the pictures of different people who had graced the ranch with their presence, and the large wood posts that frame the doorway leading into the main lodge area made this place home.

"We take meals in here. Breakfast is at eight, lunch at twelve-thirty and dinner at five-thirty. They will clang a dinner bell outside to call you when meals are being served."

"Sound good."

"I hope there aren't too many people on the ranch to bother you while you're here. If we would have had a little more notice, we might have been able to accommodate your privacy more."

"It's fine, Jackson. I don't mind, really."

"You say so now, but if you're mobbed, it will be a whole different story."

She smiled as she skimmed her palm across his jaw. "Everything will be fine. We just have to work on convincing everyone we are a couple so we can get this ruse out on the road."

"Do we need to hire security for the ranch while you're here?"

"I don't think so. I'm sure you and your brothers can handle whatever comes."

"Probably."

She blew out a breath. "I just wish I knew who this psycho was so I could get on with my life. It's so hard not knowing who to be afraid of."

"I can imagine, but you're safe here."

"Thanks. I appreciate your family doing this for me. You especially."

"I haven't done anything yet."

"But you will."

"I want to help."

"I know." She leaned in to kiss him on the cheek.

Nina walked through the doorway leading back to her office. "Oh, there you are! I was beginning to wonder about you."

"Sorry, Mom. I didn't mean to make you stay up so late."

"It's fine. I haven't been sleeping well lately anyway. Too much going on." She extended her hand.

"You must be Samantha Harris. I'm Nina Young. It's nice to meet you."

Samantha stepped away from him and took his mother's hand. "And you. I want to thank you for doing this for me. I can't imagine how much of a pain this will be for you all."

"Oh, no problem at all. We've had a few celebrities here over the years. I wish we would have had a little more notice. I could have provided you with more security."

"It's fine. I doubt anyone will even notice me."

"I doubt it. You are a very popular young lady."

"Thank you."

"Jackson can show you where your room is. I thought you might be more comfortable in one of cabins so you'll have the privacy. I blocked the room next to yours so we don't rent it out to a family with rambunctious kids or something."

"You didn't have to do that. I love kids."

Nina glanced at him, making him blush. He could see the wheels turning in his mother's brain without even looking. "Great. We do have a few around here with all these boys marrying and having babies. It's great to have so many of my grandkids close."

"I bet you love it."

"Oh definitely." His mother glanced sideways at him as he shook his head. "Anyway, let me get your credit card and I'll retrieve the keys for your cabin."

"That would be great." Samantha retrieved her card from the purse on her shoulder before handing it to his mother.

"Follow me. We'll get you settled in a jiffy."

Jackson shook his head as he followed Samantha and his mother toward the office. If he knew his mother, she had plans already running through her mind. He would have to put a stop to that right away. *I can't. We need to convince the family we are a couple so I can get this crazy nutcase off Samantha's trail. Which will totally play right into Mom's hands. Damn it.*

Several moments later, Samantha was all set with her room key in hand.

"Jackson can show you where it is."

"Thanks. He already directed my bus driver to where to park the bus."

"Great." Nina rocked back on her boot heels as she stuffed her hands in the front pocket of her jeans. "Well, I will bid you two goodnight. Things start up early around here." She pointed at Jackson. "Don't forget, you have ride duty in the morning."

"Thanks for the reminder. I'd forgotten I had early horseback rides."

"There is a group going in the morning too. About nine, I believe, with some new riders."

"Is Joey around?"

"He'll be out there to help you. He already knows the drill."

"Thanks, Mom." He watched as his mother waved before she retreated down the hall to his parents' private quarters. "Shall we?" he asked, tipping his head to the side to indicated heading back out the doors to show her where her cabin stood.

"Sure."

He took her hand in his again, leading her through the lodge and back out the door. "This way."

"Oh, I need to grab some things from my bus."

"Okay." He detoured to the left, between the hitching posts not in use anymore, to the spot around the back where the bus had been parked. The driver stood leaning against the side.

"I need a ride back to town, Sam."

"Sure, Mark. I'm sure we can get a taxi out here to pick you up."

"Not this late at night," Jackson responded. "I'll take him back to town as soon as you are settled."

"Thanks, Jackson," she replied.

"I have a flight out in the morning for home, Sam. I'll fly back in when you're ready to roll again or before, if you need me."

His pointed look in Jackson's direction made the hair rise on his arms. Was the man thinking he would get in between Jackson and Samantha? Was he Sam's stalker? It would make sense since the man was close to her all the time driving the bus. "Problem, Mark?"

"Nope. Just letting her know I'm here for her should she need me. We've known each other a long time, you know."

"I can imagine."

"Stop this pissing contest, you two. Nothing will come of it." She laid her hand on Mark's arm as he turned to face her. "I'm fine. I'll be staying here with Jackson and his family for a couple of weeks. You go on home. I'll call you when I need you to fly back."

"Sure, Sam. Be careful, huh? I wouldn't want you to get hurt."

"I won't, but thanks."

Samantha opened the door to the bus before she climbed the three stairs into the interior. Jackson hesitated a minute, giving Mark a look he hoped said back off as he followed her inside and shut the door behind them.

"I'll just grab a few things. Be out in a minute."

"Okay." Jackson took a seat on the couch to the left as he waited for Samantha to return. He could hear the banging of drawers coming from the back of the bus. *Women. They were so needy sometimes.*

About thirty minutes later, she opened the door to the back part of the bus, rolling three suitcases with her. "Jesus, woman. What the hell do you have in there? Not like you couldn't come back in here anytime to retrieve more stuff."

"I know, but I didn't want to forget anything. One is my hair stuff, makeup, shampoo and all that jazz, one has my shoes, and the other one has my clothes."

"You have one suitcase for just shoes?"

"Oh yeah. I have to have sandals, heels, boots, flip-flops, high-heeled boots, low-heeled boots, high-heel dress shoes, low-heel dress shoes. A woman can never have enough shoes."

"Apparently." He shook his head as he reached for one of the cases to carry it down the stairs. The damn thing weighed about a hundred pounds.

When he had her and her suitcases on the ground, he grabbed one in each hand and headed for the cabin in the distance. He was kind of glad his mother put her near his. It would make getting this whole charade started much easier. *I'm not sure how much of a charade it is since I totally want to get her into my bed.* "Follow me."

"Right." She grabbed the smallest of the three and waved to Mark, before following him the several yards to the front of her cabin.

He liked this particular set of rooms on the property out of all the cabins set aside for guests. It had a small porch running across the front where guests could sit outside, sip coffee or something and watch the sunrise. Big wooden posts held up the porch, providing a railing should you want to hitch a horse to one of them. Two rocking chairs made out of cedar sat near each other with a small table between them. The doors on the cabins were made of solid oak and were very heavy to move. The inside had a large, king size bed with a handmade quilt over the top, hand-sewn curtains on the windows to match the pattern on the quilt, pictures of several different kinds of flowers gracing the walls, and beautiful throw rugs gracing the wooden floors.

"I think you'll like these rooms. There is a door between the two in case you have someone come out who you might want to use the other room."

"I don't know who would do that."

"Maybe you could invite your parents out. I think that would be cool."

She tapped her fingers on her lips as she took in the space around them. "What a great idea. My mom and dad could sure use a vacation away. My sisters can tend the animals for a few days." She gave him a beautiful smile. "Thanks, Jackson."

"No problem." He shoved his hands in his pockets to keep from reaching for her. He wanted to touch her, stroke her skin, run his fingers through her hair to see if he could get her to make sweet little noises as he brought her to the peak of ecstasy.

To keep himself from actually doing what he wanted to do, he let his thoughts drift to other things like if she was an early riser. He figured probably not since she always had to be up late performing. It would be interesting to find out little tidbits about her while she took the two weeks off on the ranch with him.

"Well, I should get going so I can take Mark back to San Antonio, plus I have rides to run in the morning."

"Do you all have a gym on site?"

"Yeah, upstairs in the main lodge there is equipment. Take the stairs to the back of the dining room to the second floor, turn left. It's in the back. There is a treadmill, elliptical, weights, and a couple exercise balls."

"Sounds perfect."

"I guess I'll see you tomorrow at breakfast."

"Goodnight."

"Night, Jackson. Sleep well."

\* \* \* \*

Samantha slowly closed the door behind Jackson, watching him for several minutes before she got the panel completely closed. She really did like him, a lot. He had the sexy thing down, gorgeous, and those arms, wow. She'd give just about anything to be held in those arms. The muscles of his biceps bulged nicely every time he moved. His chest was something she could get lost in if he hugged her tight. Hugs were the best if they were from the right guy. She really liked how he wore his facial hair. Trimmed nicely, he wore it framing his face along his jawline, a mustache above his lips, and down in almost a goatee style, but only on the edge of his chin. It looked great on him.

She sighed heavily as she backed away from the door, almost tripping over the suitcases left next to the bed. The room screamed country chic with its homey décor, pretty coverlet on the bed, and the nice dried flowers sitting on the nightstand. She could get used to this.

After glancing at the clock and realizing how late it had become, she tossed the biggest suitcase on the bed. She needed something to sleep in.

The roar of Jackson's truck drew her to the window looking out over the front lawn. She watched as he backed out and slowly drove down the gravel driveway to take Mark back to town. Jackson really was a great guy, the kind she could definitely like for longer than a few days.

"Well, bed it is." She returned to the bed, opened the suitcase and pulled out a pair of shorts and a tank top. When she got changed, she put the suitcase on the floor at the bottom of the bed. She needed her smaller one with her toiletries in it so she could brush her teeth and comb out her hair before braiding it for bed. If she didn't tie it back, a wild mess would greet her come morning.

When she had everything in place, she slid beneath the fresh sheets on the bed, and leaned over to flip off the light before she snuggled down under the covers. The bed seemed comfortable and plenty big enough for two. She sighed as she closed her eyes, waiting for sleep to claim her. Her thoughts drifted to Jackson and their conversation on the bus. Was she really an alcoholic? She didn't think so at all. Yeah, she had a few drinks before she performed, sometimes a little vodka in her coffee or a drink before bed, but she could go without the booze anytime she wanted to. *Nah.* She would show him. She wouldn't drink at all while she stayed on his family's ranch. Alcohol didn't mean that much to her. She only used it to calm her nerves at various times during the day when she felt stressed out. Nothing big, right? Right.

She exhaled on a rush, pulling covers up to her ears. As she drifted off to sleep, her dreams filled with thoughts of Jackson and what he could do to bring her to the heights of ecstasy.

*He stood at her door in nothing but his jeans, his boots, and his cowboy hat.*

*"Can I come in?"*

*"Of course."*

*He stepped across the threshold and swept her up in his arms, crushing his mouth against hers. His tongue danced along the seam of her lips using small licks, until she opened to his probing. Her body tingled as their tongues dueled from her mouth to his and back. His hands swept down her back, instantly cupping her ass in both of his palms and dragging her up against his chest. His mouth left hers to skim over her cheek, nipping at her jawline as he went, before he reached her ear to slip the lobe between his teeth too. God, she loved a man with a talented mouth.*

*"I want you, Samantha."*

*"Oh yeah."*

*"You are everything a man wants in a woman, bold, sexy, daring, and gorgeous beyond words. I want to eat you until you scream my name. Then I'm going to fuck you so hard, you'll have to brace yourself for the onslaught of feelings racing through you with every thrust of my hips."*

*"Yes."*

*He bent down and swept her up in his arms before he moved toward the bed to deposit her in the middle. Two fingers hooked in her underwear, slowly peeled them down her legs and tossed them over his shoulder to somewhere on the floor. She laid there in nothing but one of his dress shirts buttoned up the front. "I'll get to those gorgeous nipples in a minute. Right now, I need to taste you."*

*Seconds later, his head disappeared between her thighs. The first swipe of his tongue almost brought her out of her skin. "Oh, God."*

*She tossed his hat across the comforter on the bed. Winding her hands into the hair on the top of his head, she held him tight against her pussy. Good grief, he had a talented tongue. Each swipe, each lick, each nibble brought her higher until she couldn't help tossing her head as he ate at her like a starving man. The whiskers on his chin scraped her flesh, abrading it deliciously as he continued to suck at her clit.*

*"Come for me, Samantha."*

*The sharp sting of a bite on her clit threw her into the most amazing orgasm she'd ever had. Lights danced behind her closed eyelids as she screamed his name when he drove two fingers into her pussy, throwing her over the climatic abyss again.*

Samantha bolted upright in the bed. Her heart pounded so hard against her chest, she thought she might be having a heart attack. Her breath came out in a ragged seesaw of sounds until realization hit. The whole thing had all been a dream. Jackson wasn't with her making her come so hard she thought she might die.

"Holy shit."

Her pussy ached with a need she couldn't fulfill in the way she wanted to more than anything on this earth at the moment.

"I need a shower. I'd better make it a cold one."

She whipped the covers back, sliding her legs over the edge of the bed before she stood up. Moonlight drifted through the curtains at the front of the cabin, lighting her way to the unfamiliar bathroom. When she flipped on the light, she blinked several times to bring the room into focus. The space sparkled. There were subway titles in black lining all the walls including the fully enclosed shower. Silver accents accompanied everything. A silver framed mirror hung over the white sink with old-fashioned porcelain handles to turn on the hot and cold water. The only other color in the room was the royal blue rugs on the floor and a shower curtain with royal blue flowers. *Breathtaking.*

She turned on the shower before stripping off her clothes and standing beneath the spray. The water cascaded over her shoulders, working away the knots her dream had placed there, with its warmth.

*This isn't going to cut it. I need to get off.*

She lifted her foot onto the bench seat along the back wall of the shower, sliding her fingers through the curls at the apex of her thighs. Her clit was still slick with her juices from her all too vivid dream of Jackson eating her out.

Her whole body hummed from not being satisfied like she craved.

She quickly began working her clit with her fingertips, rubbing first one side, then the other, hovering on the brink of coming. She let herself get lost in the memory of the dream again. As sensory overload took over, her body bowed tight and she came on a rush. Too bad the self-satisfaction paled in comparison to her dream

Feeling almost unsatisfied to the point of exhaustion, she turned the water off before grabbing a towel to dry her body. She stepped out of the shower, and then padded softly across the wooden floor in her bare feet.

She's almost reached the bed when she heard a soft knock on the door.

Frozen in fear, she wasn't sure whether she should answer or not until she heard a voice she recognized calling her name through the panel.

# Chapter Four

"Samantha, are you okay?" Jackson tapped on the door when he saw the light on in her cabin after he'd returned from taking her bus driver back to San Antonio. He wanted to make sure she didn't need anything.

When she opened the door, he almost swallowed his tongue. She stood in front of him in nothing more than a large towel wrapped around her gorgeous frame.

"I'm fine, Jackson." She tossed her hair over her shoulder as she tugged the towel a little closer around her body. "I just took a shower before bed, is all."

"Okay. I saw your light on. I wanted to make sure you didn't need anything." *Like me needing to run my tongue all over your body, licking up every little droplet of water I see.* He swallowed hard. His cock slowly began to fill, pressing on the zipper of his jeans.

She glanced down, and then back up to meet his gaze. One eyebrow rose over her right eye.

"You're standing here in nothing, but a towel. What did you expect to happen?"

She moved a little closer, close enough he could smell the scent of her body wash on her skin. "Do you want to come in?"

"Hell yes, I do, but I don't think that's such a good idea."

"Why?"

"Because you are standing there in nothing but a towel."

"Yeah, I know."

The lump in his throat felt like it would choke him if he swallowed again, but the saliva pooling in his mouth didn't give him much choice in the matter. He stepped forward, bringing her so her breasts brushed his chest. "This is a bad idea."

"I don't think so."

"I do. My mom has a rule against the boys messing with guests."

"I'm not a guest."

"You're not?"

"Well, technically, yes, but we are supposed to be getting to the point where we can convince your family and everyone else, we are a couple."

"And?"

"What if we really are?"

"Do you want to be?"

"I don't know." Her gaze swept over him from head to the toes of his boots. "You're kind of cute with all your cowboyness."

The towel slipped a hair, gaping open in the front around her breasts. Water glistened on her skin, making him wonder if she was cold standing there in the cooler evening air. Maybe he should walk her backward into the room, you know, just for propriety sake. "You make it sound like a disease or something."

"Not at all. If you hadn't noticed, I like cowboys."

"I hadn't noticed."

She laughed as she adjusted the towel.

"Aren't you cold?"

"Yeah, a little."

"I'll leave you to get ready for bed then."

Her bottom lip came out in a pout. "I hoped you'd help me, you know, get dressed or undressed as the case may be."

He would be in hell come morning for lying to her about wanting her right now. "I think it would be better if we waited on that score."

"You don't want to have sex with me?"

"I didn't say I didn't want to have sex with you."

"What's the problem then?"

"Why don't we leave that for when we know each other a bit better?"

She took a step back, readjusting the towel to cover a little more. "Wow. I've never had a guy turn down sex before. This is a first."

"I think it would be a whole lot better if we knew each other a little more beforehand, that's all. I think you're a real nice gal, but I think I'd like to know you a bit before we had sex." He adjusted himself in his jeans. "Not that I don't want you, because yeah, I do. You're a beautiful woman with all the assets I like, but I think it would make things a little awkward should we have sex now, and then try to convince everyone we are having sex, when we might not be in the future." He raked his fingers through his hair, before adjusting his hat back on his head. "Does anything I just said make any sense at all?"

"Sure, Jackson."

She shrugged although the look on her face told him she didn't really understand how he could turn her down.

"I'll see you in the morning at breakfast."

"Of course, thanks for checking on me. I appreciate it."

"You're welcome." She moved to shut the door as he stepped back off the porch. "Night."

"Goodnight."

* * * *

Morning came too damned early for Jackson as he rolled over to punch his pillow for umpteenth time since he'd went to bed. He'd spent the night rolling from one side of the bed to the other because of one blonde beauty who had wound his dick tight enough to shoot the eye out of a cow with his cum should he have let go. Now, his balls ached with need and he'd shut her down to the point where he didn't know if he'd get any or not.

A rousting knock sounded on his door.

"Jackson?"

*Samantha*. His dick hadn't softened all damned night long, but it was straight up and begging at the sound of her voice.

"I'll be right there."

He jumped out of bed, hitting his toe on the footboard. "Fucking son of a bitch!"

"Are you all right?"

"Yeah. I hit my toe. I'll be there in a second. I need to put some clothes on."

"Don't get dressed on my account."

He needed a shower, cold one preferably, but he didn't have time.

The bell clanged for breakfast.

Late again.

His toe throbbed with every beat of his heart as he limped to his dresser to retrieve some clean clothes. His boots were going to kill him to put on, plus he had to take the group out this morning on the horses. Maybe he could get Joey to take his ride. He hoped he hadn't broken his toe. It hurt like the devil.

Once he had his clothes on, he opened the door to find Samantha decked out in a sexy pair of jeans and a long-sleeved blouse that button down the front in a pretty, solid pink fabric with embroidered flowers on the shoulders. A straw cowboy hat graced her head, covering her blonde hair except for the long straight strands cascading down her back. He wanted nothing more than to touch the silky looking mane.

"You look fresh and rested this morning."

She gave him a once over from his head to his boots. "You look like shit."

"Thanks."

"You're welcome." She bounced on her booted toes, shuffling her feet a little in her haste to be gone. "I thought you could walk me to breakfast. We need to start this little facade of ours sooner rather than later."

"I know, but I'd better warn you about my mother and her matchmaking skills."

"Matchmaking?"

"She'll have us paired whether we want to be or not before the end of the day. She's done that with all of my brothers so far. She's done a pretty good job of picking out their mate for them even if it took them a while to figure things out, but I don't want her to get her hopes up about us. This isn't real or at least not from my end."

She stepped back as he shut the door behind him.

"I know it's not real, Jackson. We are playing a role. It's like acting in a movie or something. We are playing a couple so we can catch this crazy person who is stalking me. We do have to make everything look convincing though."

"I don't want my family hurt in this ruse."

"They won't be."

"I'm not so sure."

She made a cross over her heart. "I promise to do my best not to hurt your family in this."

"What about your family?"

"Unless for some reason we make a trip to Iowa, they don't even need to know about us."

"What if the news reporters pick up on this charade and broadcast it all over the country music news? They'll see it then."

She tapped her fingers to her lips for a moment. "Well, we'll have to make up some kind of excuse why we broke up. Thing like this happen in this business all the time. It won't be a surprise to anyone."

"You aren't taking this very seriously."

"I'm dead serious, Jackson. I need to get this psycho away from me. I'm afraid, terrified really, and it would make me feel a lot better having you around."

She definitely knew how to play on his emotions about women in general. Yeah, he liked to fuck them from here to tomorrow, but let one be in trouble, and he would be right there to help. Damn chivalry. "Let's get some breakfast, shall we? We'll worry about the other later."

She fell into step beside him as they made their way toward the main lodge. "What kind of food to do you like?"

"Everything."

"Like?"

"I'm a meat and potatoes kind of guy, I guess, but one of my weaknesses is cookies."

"What kind of cookies?"

"Chocolate chip specifically, but I love oatmeal with raisins too."

As their hands brushed together during their walk, she grabbed his in hers, holding on tightly as she laced their fingers together. When he shot her a look, she just smiled as she snuggled closer to his side. This façade of a relationship was going to kill him sooner rather than later if he didn't die from blue balls or guilt first.

When they walked through the doors of the big house, he directed her toward the line of people getting their food. "Go ahead and get your plate. The family always waits until everyone else is served."

"I'll wait for you."

"Do you want to sit over here near the door?"

"Where do you usually sit?" she asked, leaning into his arm so her breasts pressed against him.

"With my family at those two long tables near the stairs."

The whole table of people turned to stare as he and Samantha made their way inside the room. Was it that unusual for him to have a woman by his side? No, but it was different for him to bring one home, so to speak. He didn't do the girlfriend thing and he didn't think Samantha did the simpering female thing either, so she better knock this shit off.

He slowly disengaged his arm from her grasp. The pout on her lips made him want to kiss her, which seemed to be her reasoning behind it so he resisted with everything inside him. As they approached the table, the family fell silent. "Everyone, this is Samantha Harris for those of you who don't know her. Ya'll probably saw her bus out back. She's staying for a couple of weeks in one of the cabins to relax before she hits the road." He went around the table introducing everyone present, skipping those who already knew her, before he found them two seats at the end of the table to the next to Joshua and Candace.

Samantha gave him a blinding smile over her shoulder, as he held out her chair for her. "Thank you."

"You're welcome." He gripped the seatback of the chair next to her. "Can I get you some coffee or juice?"

"Coffee would be great."

"Be right back." His brothers all stared as he made his way toward the large coffee pot sitting to the left in the corner. He knew they had to play this up for everything it was worth, but he wasn't sure exactly how to go about it. How did one treat a girlfriend verses a one-night stand? He wasn't sure. He'd never had a girlfriend per se except in high school and you couldn't really call that a girlfriend. *Okay, be cool. Do things for her like get her plate, hold her chair, open the door, all the things Ma taught us as boys in how to be a gentleman. Good start.*

The conversation from the table drifted to his ears as he poured two cups of coffee, added cream and sugar to his before gathering some for Samantha.

"Are you really Samantha Harris the country music star?" Paige asked.

"Yes."

"I love your music."

"Thank you. I'm thrilled to hear that. I love meeting fans."

"I'm a huge one."

"You can say that again," Jacob added. "She has all your stuff on her iPod."

"I appreciate the support."

"Do you travel a lot?" This came from Mesa.

"Yeah. When we are on tour, we are gone for several weeks without much of a break."

"I bet it's hard being gone all the time."

"Yes, although I'm used to it by now. The bus has all the amenities. It's like living in a small apartment."

"Nice."

"Do you play an instrument like an acoustic guitar?" Joey's voice carried to Jackson's ears from the end of the table.

"Some. I rely a lot on the guys in the band to carry the music. I do write some of my own songs though, so I do have to play a little to be able to do that."

"She plays beautifully. Don't let her fool you," Candace added before she took a sip of her juice. "I've heard her play many times."

It was Samantha's turn to ask a question. "Did any of you come out for the benefit concert last night?"

Several of his brothers nodded affirmatively as well as voiced their pleasure at her performance, but Jeff replied, "You did awesome, Samantha."

When Jackson returned to the table, he noticed the blush on her cheeks. She really didn't know how to handle her fame very well if she turned red at the smallest compliments. He set the cup down in front of her with the cream and sugar, loving how she glanced up as a pretty smile spread across her lips.

Thoughts of leaning in to give her a quick kiss raced across his mind until Jeff started talking about guests coming in, how many they had on the place now, horses needing to be broke, rides needing guides, and more ranch stuff.

Jackson took the seat next to Samantha, sipping the steaming hot liquid in his cup slowly so he didn't burn his mouth, until time for them to get their own plates of food. Samantha got quiet while the rest of the group picked up the slack in the conversations going around the table. "You okay?"

"Yes, why?"

"I don't want you to be overwhelmed with my family. They can be a bit rough on newcomers to the group."

"They are great. I wish I had a big family. I really would love to sit down to talk to your mother about raising all of you. I bet she has some great stories."

"I'm sure."

"Where are you in the pecking order?"

"Second to the eldest. Jeff is the eldest, then me, Jacob, Jason, Joel, Joshua are the triplets, Jonathan, Jeremiah and last is Joey."

"And the only ones not paired off?"

"Me, Jonathan and Joey. Everyone else has a steady girl, married or getting married soon as in Candace and Joshua's case." The group surged to their feet in a large wave as his mother gave the signal for them to get their own plates. "We can eat now."

"Is it always like this?"

"Like what?" he asked, pulling out her chair for her.

"A huge wave of people heading to the food line." She giggled and fell into step beside him as they headed toward the back of the line.

"Yep."

Those of his brothers paired off, who already had children to care for, usually fixed their spouse's plates for them while the women managed the various highchairs hanging around the room. Jacob and Paige had twins, Jeff and Terri had three kids now, Joel and Mesa had their daughter, and the news had broken around the family in the last couple of weeks that they were expecting again. The family had grown exponentially over the last few years with the addition of the women and children. He smiled when he thought about it. His mom was in heaven with all these grandkids and women around after raising nine boys, plus the newest addition coming soon to Joel and Mesa.

"What are you smiling about?"

"Just thinking about my mom with all of her grandkids and daughters-in-law around her. After having nothing but boys, she's ecstatic now and totally in her element."

Samantha glanced over her shoulder as Nina snuggled one of her grandkids on her hip, making the child giggle hysterically. Lucky for all of them, Nina had recovered fully from her car accident a few months ago, that had left her with a broken leg. Time had stood still for all of them that night as they wondered if she would be okay in the long run. Not only had she broke her leg, but she'd had a bleed on her brain when some guy had hit her head on when she was headed to town in one of the ranch trucks.

He really did love his family even though they got on his nerves sometimes.

Nina shot a look his way with a little chin tip in Samantha's direction as a grin graced her lips. His mother was playing matchmaker already. He knew the signs. He hoped she didn't get hurt in this scam they were playing.

As the two of them approached the serving containers, he saw Mandy across the table from him. "Hey, Mandy. This is—"

"Samantha Harris," Mandy gushed a little. "I absolutely love your music. I'm glad you came to the ranch to chill out. I promise I won't bug you."

Samantha laughed. "It's nice to meet you."

"Oh my gosh. You too." Mandy put some eggs on Samantha's plate along with a couple of pieces of bacon. "I hope you enjoy your stay here."

"I'm sure I will."

Mandy motioned with the tongs. "Are you and Jackson like, you know, a couple?"

"Sort of." Samantha grinned in his direction. "We are at the 'get to know you phase'."

"Awesome. He's a great guy. All of the boys are."

"Especially Jonathan." Jackson loved teasing her about her crush on his brother. Jonathan seemed to be the only one who didn't know about her true feelings.

"Yeah, him too."

Samantha frowned as they continued through the line. "Jonathan?"

"Yeah. Mandy has a serious crush going on with him, but he seems to be oblivious to her feelings."

"Well that sucks."

"Yeah."

With their plates now full, they headed back to their seats at the table. He'd have to watch his manners around Samantha. She probably had that kind of thing down pat and he didn't want to look like a heathen shoveling food into his mouth. When he started to care about it, he wasn't sure, but yeah, it seemed the thing to do.

The conversations flowed around them as the table occupants ate, laughed, and sipped their coffee before chores began for the day.

"Jackson, you're on escort duty this morning."

"Yeah, I know."

"There are seven riders unless Samantha wants to go. You can take the group by yourself. I don't think you need a second. Everyone riding is experienced, the new riders backed out earlier."

"No, I think I'll work on a new song I've been kicking around for the last week or so."

"Okay. I will be gone a little over an hour."

Samantha nodded before taking a sip of her coffee. "I'll be here checking out the property or something."

"Sounds good."

Jeff went around the table making sure everyone had their assignments for the day or at least those of the boys who did the physical labor around the ranch. Jeremiah did the financial stuff and Jonathan concentrated on the computer graphics as well as the website marketing.

"Grandma is babysitting all the munchkins while the girls go out to the spa today," Mesa added with a grin.

"I'm game," was the chorus of female agreement around the table as Nina held up her hands and shook her head with an emphatic no way.

"Well damn." Mesa laughed. "I thought for sure we could slip our plans by you, Grandma."

Nina laughed. "I have my own work to do, girls. You'll have to hire babysitters if you want a day at the spa."

"I'm lucky enough Elizabeth still takes naps."

"Yeah, not me with these two," Paige added as she glanced at her two in the corner making a huge mess on the floor with their food. They were working on their fine motor skills with the utensils, but they were still learning. Paige took the spoon and turned it around in Hannah's hand. "It's faster that way, Hannah." Hannah just giggled as she banged the spoon on the highchair.

In turn, Josiah did the same thing. "No, Hannah. No Josiah," Paige scolded.

Jackson shook his head as he sipped his coffee. He didn't want kids, at least not yet anyway. He was perfectly fine being a bachelor although he had to admit his clock ticked relentlessly. *How old is Samantha?* He wasn't sure, but he thought she might be in her mid to late twenties, which made her quite a bit younger than his own age. Didn't matter. She was one hell of a pretty woman any way you sliced it.

He glanced at his watch. It was close enough to nine, he needed to get out to the barn to get ready for the group going out this morning. After he drained his cup, he stood. "I'll catch you later, Sam. I need to get out to the barn."

"Sure. I'll hang out here for a bit or whatever. I'm sure there is plenty to do around a working ranch. I don't expect you to take time off to entertain me. I can handle myself just fine."

"Good. See you after while."

"Have fun."

He headed for the door with her gaze fixed on his back. He could feel her look without even glancing behind him. They were attracted to each other, no doubt about that, but what would come of the attraction, he didn't know. Did he want to make this ruse real? Maybe. He sure would like to fuck her. What would it be like living with her on her bus for several weeks, making love to her on a regular basis as they traveled around the country waiting for her stalker to make a move?

As he made his way outside, the thought became more and more intriguing. This might be just the distraction he needed in his life.

# Chapter Five

Samantha watched as Jackson headed out the door. *Damn, he's got a nice ass in those jeans.* Not one to ignore or under-appreciate a man's assets, she couldn't help but notice he sported quite the package in the front too. *Maybe thoughts like those aren't very nice to have sitting at the table with his family.*

"What are your plans, Sam," Nina asked.

"I'm not sure. I have some work I can be doing on my bus like writing on this song I have playing over and over in my head. I can check in with my agent. I can clean the mess on the bus. But what I'd really like to do is make some cookies."

"Make cookies?"

"Yeah. Jackson said his favorite was chocolate chip. Do you mind if I make him some?"

The whole family grinned as a few of them laughed. "Not at all. In fact, I believe we have everything in the kitchen to make them, but check with the cook. We haven't had homemade chocolate chip cookies around here in a while. He will really appreciate them, I'm sure. He's a sucker for desserts."

Samantha smiled. The way to get to the man was through his stomach, eh? Well, that's one thing her momma taught her, to cook up a storm, and desserts were her favorite too. She drank the last bit of her coffee, and then stood. "I'm going to do some things on my bus for a bit before I tackle the cookies. That should give them time to clean up from breakfast before I destroy their kitchen again."

The family laughed. It was a good feeling to be around. She missed her parents and her sisters. They were all a bit younger than she was by a few years even though they all had their own lives these days.

When she'd hit it big, she'd paid off her parents' farm, given her sisters some money so they could go to school or whatever they wanted to do, then sat on the rest. She did give to several charities over the years including many who took care of children. She loved kids although she didn't want any of her own for now. Her biological clock had started ticking at a pretty fast pace these days as her own age pushed thirty. She nodded to the group before walking toward the door. Her bus sat around back of the main lodge where Mark had parked it when they came in last night.

Cleaning wasn't her forte, but she realized she needed to straighten up the bus a bit from her frantic throwing together a bag after they'd arrived at the ranch. Even though it was close and she could grab what she wanted, she didn't want to spend a lot of time on the bus. She already spent way too much time on there while traveling. Being on the ranch with Jackson meant relaxation at its finest, and she meant to do exactly that, relax.

When she reached the front of the huge monstrosity she called home most days, she opened the door before taking the few steps up to reach the living space. She took in the clothes strewn across the couch, her customary cowboy hat sitting on the back of the sofa, her boots on the floor, her makeup bag with the majority of her cosmetics on the counter, and the overall appearance of the space. "What a pigsty." She grabbed the clothes and boots before walking back toward her bedroom to toss the offending garments in the dirty clothes bin. She would have to throw some things in the washer since the basket almost overflowed. Washing clothes was one of the tolerable chores she had to do.

A few minutes later, she returned to the front of the bus, spotting the half-empty whiskey bottle sitting on the counter in the kitchen. Nine in the morning wasn't too early for a little drink. It would relax her so she could clean and not notice the work involved. She unscrewed the top on the bottle to pour enough to fill the tumbler half full. Next, she grabbed her iPod, plugged in the headphones, clipped it on her belt and began to clean.

After over an hour of straightening up her bus, she sat down with her guitar, the sheet of paper she'd been writing the new song on and plucked out a few chords. The words started to flow from her mind to her fingers as the song took shape. What she'd written impressed her. The song sounded good. She knew that, but she still had doubts, always doubts.

She glanced over to the bottle on the counter, realizing the entire thing had disappeared when she went to pour another glass. *When did that happen? Oh well. I feel fine.* She stood and her head swam. *Wow. Maybe I'm a little drunk.* She glanced at the clock on the microwave. Eleven in the morning. She'd still have time to make Jackson's cookies before they started preparing for lunch, if she hurried.

Taking the steps quickly as she could without falling, she rushed toward the main lodge. She made it through the door without too much trouble. "Hey," she said, noticing Mandy wiping down tables and preparing the room for lunch.

"Hey."

"I got tied up cleaning and song writing on the bus. Can I still make cookies?"

"Um, I guess. Check with the cook though. She's pretty possessive about her kitchen. It might be better after lunch since we have a little more time between dinner and supper." Mandy wrinkled her nose as Samantha stepped closer.

"Oh, that's sounds like a great plan. I'm sure for me to do enough for everyone, it will take a few hours to bake them all."

"Yeah, I'm sure it will."

"I will check with the cook." Samantha slowly made her way toward the double swinging doors leading into the kitchen. Her boots seemed like they were wet or something, making it hard to lift her feet. It took two tries for her to get through the doorway into the back part of the kitchen where the cook, Millie, stood over the countertop making patties out of raw hamburger. "Hi, Millie?"

Millie turned toward her with a smile on her lips and a twinkle in her eyes. "Yes, ma'am?"

"Nina said I could talk to you about making some chocolate chips cookies for everyone, but especially Jackson."

"That boy does like his dessert."

She laughed. "So I hear."

Millie's eyebrows drew down as her lips formed a frown. Samantha wondered why the cook's demeanor changed. "It's getting too close to lunch to do it now."

"Mandy mentioned after lunch."

"I suppose it would be okay. I can be here to supervise."

"Oh, no need for that. I love to cook, and I'm great in the kitchen."

"Really?"

"Yes, ma'am."

Millie gave her a look like she didn't believe her. "I'd still feel much better if I were here with you. I can show you where everything is and so on."

"I'd much rather cook alone."

"I will check with Ms. Nina, but if that is your wish, so be it."

"Thank you. I'll be back right after lunch is over to get started. Thank you."

Samantha spun on her heels to return to the front of the dining area, wobbling slightly as she walked. *I need some coffee or something. I sure didn't realize I'd drank half a bottle. That's even a bit much for me.*

She waved at Mandy as she made her way back out toward her bus. She had about ninety minutes before lunch from what Jackson said, so she'd just get a little more work done on her song.

When she sat down again with her guitar, she plucked a few strings but it didn't sound right. Something seemed off, but she wasn't sure what. She glanced at the empty bottle again. *A little more wouldn't hurt anything. I seemed to be writing better with a little alcohol in me.* After she searched the cupboards above the sink, she found another full bottle of Jack Daniel's. With a smile on her lips, she poured half a tumbler, sat down with her guitar and the glass in her hand, trying to get comfortable.

The words and chords came much easier as she sipped the brown liquid.

Before she knew it, the lunch bell clanged, jarring her from her thoughts. She grabbed the glass on the table, downed the rest of the alcohol and then stood, setting her guitar on the couch near where she'd been sitting.

Her lips and mouth were as dry as the dessert. She needed water to wet her parched mouth and take away the pasty feeling.

She ran her fingers through her long tresses, trying to straighten out the strands to make herself presentable for lunch. Her stomach grumbled. Food sounded awfully good right now even though it really hadn't been that long since breakfast.

What had Jackson been doing all morning after his ride? She giggled as she pressed her fingertips to her lips. *I'd like to ride him into next week.* "Maybe later if I can get him to cooperate a little."

She blew out a breath, realizing she needed to brush her teeth quickly.

Several minutes later, she stumbled through the door to the main lodge, drawing all eyes to her entrance. Heat flushed her cheeks. She hated making a scene, but that's exactly what she'd done.

Jackson quickly moved to her side. "Are you okay? You didn't trip over the stoop or anything we need to check, did you?"

"No, I'm fine. I tripped over my own two feet is all."

Jackson's eyes narrowed. "Have you been drinking, Sam?"

"No. I was cleaning and writing all morning. Why?"

"You smell like alcohol."

"It's probably the rubbing alcohol I used to clean my makeup brushes."

"On your breath?"

She pushed out of his reach. "I'm not drunk, Jackson."

"I didn't say you were."

"Then stop acting like my keeper. I'm a grown adult. I can do what I want." She moved toward the serving line, not waiting for him or his family. *To hell with him and his judgmental ass.* She would get her food and eat alone. Not like she hadn't been alone before.

Once she filled her plate, she grabbed a Coke from the ice bin, before taking a seat near the door. While she lifted a forkful of potato salad to her lips, she watched Jackson retrieve his own plate of food from the serving line. She wished she knew why she liked him so much or why she was so attracted to his condescending ass.

He reached the end of the line, grabbed a soda from the bin, and then turned to walk in her direction. "Mind if I join you?"

"Yeah, but it's a free country. Sit wherever you want."

He took the bench seat across from her, setting his plate down on the table. "I'm sorry."

"You should be."

"Sam, I am not judging you."

"You already did." She continued to eat, ignoring him as much as she could with his grey gaze studying her so hard. "Will you stop looking at me like that? Why don't you eat with your family since you're all high and mighty and don't do a damned thing wrong."

"I'm sorry. I don't think I'm better than you. I've had my problems. My family has had its problems. We aren't perfect by a long shot."

"Then why are you trying to make me sound like a drunk? I only drink when I need it, which isn't very often."

"Did you drink this morning?"

"None of your business."

"If I'm supposed to be your boyfriend, I'm making it my business."

"Too fucking bad, Jackson, because what I do on my own time is my own. I don't need a keeper. If you think that's what this whole facade is about, then forget it. I'll find someone else to be my pretend boyfriend so I can find this crazy person stalking me. I don't need you."

He grabbed her hand as she tried to stand. "Yes, you do, Samantha. You need me a hell of a lot more than I need you, but that's beside the point. I'm going to help you whether you want me to or not."

She slowly slid back down in her seat. "You're right. I do need you."

"I know you do, and I'm going to help you."

"What do we do?"

"First we have to establish ourselves as a couple, which means spending a lot of time together. I do mean a lot."

She smiled. "I'm game."

"Not like that. Not yet."

She raked her fingernails down his arm in a slow caress. "What did you have in mind?"

"You can help me with chores around here. We always need someone to help shovel shit, groom the animals, toss hay bales, clean tack, and do paperwork."

She wrinkled her nose in disgust. After all, she was a big country music star. They don't shovel shit. "But what about my music?"

"Your music is on the backburner. For now, you are nothing more than the farm girl you were before you started making music."

She blew out a frustrated breath. "Okay."

"Good. We'll start this afternoon."

"Uh, I already have plans this afternoon."

"Doing what?"

"It's a surprise for you."

One eyebrow rose over his left eye. "A surprise?"

"Yes, and I'm not telling you what it is."

His hand still held her fingers. "Fine. We'll start first thing in the morning. I'm usually up at six. I'll expect you to be up by then too. Have you ridden horses?"

"I used to do rodeo when I was in high school."

"What event?"

"Barrels and pole bending."

"Good. You can go with me on guest rides. You can pull up the back of the herd as we go out over the mountains. It should give you plenty of time to think."

"Six?"

"Yep. I help Joey with the horses first thing in the morning. We have stalls to clean, groom the horses, and make sure they are fed before it's time to take the first group out in the morning after breakfast."

"Fine," she grumbled, using a few choice words under her breath for the taskmaster he'd become in the last few minutes. This wasn't going to be a very fun two weeks, and even worse, she made plans to take his ass on the road with her.

*What the hell was I thinking?*

As soon as they had finished their meal and put their plates in the dirty dishes bin, Jackson disappeared to do some chores around the ranch as she prepared to make his cookies. She pushed through the double doors into the kitchen to find Millie rushing about with two other helpers including Mandy, cleaning up the kitchen from lunch.

"You can use the space over there for your cookie making. I've already put out all the ingredients you'll need. Do you need a recipe?" Milly asked, with her hands on her ample hips.

The woman obviously loved to eat as much as she liked to cook from the size of her. She couldn't stand much above five foot with broad shoulders, round body and short legs. She had rounded cheeks flushed from the heat of the cook stoves in the kitchen. Her greying hair pulled back into a bun at the base of her head reminded Samantha of her grandmother.

"If you have one, that would be great. I know the ingredients but I don't remember all the exact measurements for each thing."

"I have one sitting on the counter near the flour bag for you. I've already preheated the oven. There is a cooking stone to your right you can lay them out on to bake. There is also a timer on the counter for each batch. We should be done with lunch clean up by the time you've got everything measured out and ready for the first batch."

"Thank you, Millie."

The woman wiped her hands on the apron around her middle. "You're welcome. Don't make a big mess, and make sure you clean up after yourself."

"I will."

"All right then. We'll leave you to your baking."

Samantha mixed the ingredients one by one into the bowl until it came to mixing in the chocolate chips. A few made it into her mouth before she poured the entire bag into the mixture. The dough got stiffer as she stirred.

Cooking was one of her favorite pastimes in the world. She'd always loved to cook at home, making dinners and such for her family during her childhood years. If she was upset about boys or something, she'd bake cookies, cakes, pies, rolls, muffins, cupcakes, or whatever her sweet tooth desired.

If her parents were fighting, she would make food. Whenever discord hit the family, she would cook. It was her way of dealing with the bad energy around her, she figured, but this time wasn't about baking because she was upset. Well, maybe it was a little. She didn't like fighting with Jackson. That had upset her. She could make more, but she didn't feel it was her place to take over the ranch's kitchen to assuage her nervous energy. Of course, she could always get some supplies and cook on her bus even though the kitchen wasn't very big.

Humming softly as she spooned the cookie mixture onto the baking stone Millie had provided, Samantha wondered how one of these worked. She'd never used one before, but she seen them and heard they were great for making cookies perfectly. *Hmm.* She should have asked how long to cook them for on one of these. Oh well. It should be about the same.

After she slid the stone into the preheated oven, she shut the door and put her hands on her hips. What to do for the few minutes it would take to make each batch. Maybe she should grab her guitar from the bus so she could jot down a few chords of the new song she was working on. It was really good, if she did say so herself. Being on the ranch seemed to bring out the creative side of her character.

She slipped out the double doors to head to her bus. The first batch of cookies should be ready about the time she returned as long as she didn't get sidetracked. She laughed as she imagined feeding Jackson some of the cookies. One piece at a time as the yummy morsel melted on his tongue. *What a tongue it is too.* She couldn't wait to find out how it felt on her body. It had definitely been awhile since she'd been with a man on an intimate level. Stardom had its drawbacks, definitely.

A few minutes later, she returned to the kitchen with her guitar and paper in hand. The song was almost done. It just needed something special to tweak it a hair. She wasn't quite sure what though.

The timer dinged for the cookies. When she set aside her guitar to retrieve them, she carefully put it to the right on the counter. The guitar was her favorite. It was the first one she'd bought after she got her recording contract. The white dove on the faceplate of the guitar reminded her of the one George Straight used in the movie Pure Country. She felt like him sometimes, just wanting to walk away from the whole thing without a backward glance, but she couldn't. Her family was so proud of her, she couldn't disappoint them.

With a spatula in hand, she scooped each of the cookies off the stone before putting them on the cooling plate to her left. They looked perfect, each one brown, round and gooey. As each batch took their nine minutes to cook, she wrote on the song. The soft melody and haunting chords reminded her she needed someone in her life, someone to help her with this crazy business, someone to love her for who she was, not the money she could provide for him.

So far she didn't think she'd found him, but she hadn't given Jackson a chance to prove himself yet. He seemed like a great guy with a fantastic family. They certainly didn't need her money to provide for the ranch. It looked to be a thriving business for the family with the cattle they raised, the guests they provided for, and the overall atmosphere of the ranch itself. It felt like home.

"I smell cookies."

She hopped off the barstool she'd been using to sit on. "You weren't supposed to come in here."

"How could I not. I smelled my favorite cookies. I needed to find out who loved me enough to make them today."

"Well, I don't know about love you, but I wanted to apologize for my behavior earlier so I asked the cook if I could take over the kitchen to make you chocolate chip cookies." He moved close enough she could almost drown in the grey of his eyes. When he leaned in, licking the corner of her mouth, she almost lost the ability to stand.

His breath warmed the side of her face as he skimmed his tongue from her mouth to her ear. "You had some chocolate on the corner of your mouth."

She cleared her throat nervously. "I, um." The timer dinged as she exhaled forcible. "I need to get the next batch out of the oven," she whispered. She reluctantly stepped back to turn toward the oven. With the oven mitt on her hand, she reached inside to grab the sheet and pulled them out. "Have you been a good boy?"

"Of course."

"Then I'll let you have a warm one, just one though, and only if you do something for me."

"Anything for a cookie."
"Kiss me."

# Chapter Six

Jackson's stomach flip-flopped at her whispered words. "Kiss you?" He'd wanted to do nothing more than kiss the daylights out of her since he'd met her yesterday. "I think I can handle such a small task, I mean for a warm cookie and all."

He took her by the arm, slowly turning her to face him. He framed her face with his hands. The wisps of hair caressing her cheek tickled his fingers as he slipped his hands into the hair at her temples. Her head firmly in his grasp, he tipped it back, and leaned in. He stopped a hairsbreadth away from her lips to look into the blue of her gaze. Did she want him as much as he wanted her? "Do you want me?"

"Hell yeah." Her breath whispered over his lips.

He frowned. He could still smell the alcohol mixed with toothpaste. Jacob used to be the king of masking the scent. *Benefit of the doubt is only fair.* Besides, he wanted to kiss her more than anything on this earth.

The first moment their lips touched, he could feel the heat from her mouth. She parted her lips and her tongue flicked out, licking the seam of his lips to encourage him to spar with her. He stepped closer. He needed to feel her body against his, brushing his, touching his. His dick sprang to life as he opened his mouth, drawing her deeper into the experience of their first kiss. He could drown in this experience.

Her hands wandered over his back, up and down, around to his sides where they rested on his hips. The touch of her fingers on his waist drew him further into their embrace. The experience of her mouth on his burst through his resistance to be careful with her. He couldn't help it. After all, she was Samantha Harris, the one woman he thought he'd never have.

The double doors banged against the counter. "Oh, excuse me."

He slowly lifted his head, kissing her on the nose, and then stepped back. "No problem."

"I was, uh, just finishing up the cookies. I have about one more batch to go."

"I needed to get supper started," Millie said as she stepped into the room. "Jackson, are you helping our guest make cookies?"

He swiped one of the warm ones and plopped it into his mouth. "Of course."

"I can tell." Millie moved to the huge refrigerator in the corner and began pulling out potatoes to peel. "If you really want to help, I could use a set of hands on these potatoes?"

"I, uh, have some stalls to clean."

Millie smiled as she turned to snap him with a dishtowel. "I'm sure you do."

"Ouch!" He leaned in a kissed her on the cheek. "I love you, Millie."

"I'm sure you do. Just like your brothers."

Samantha put the last batch of cookie dough into the oven. "I'll come out to help you as soon as these are done."

"Have you been writing?" he asked, noticing her guitar on the counter and the paper next to it.

"Yes, some."

"You'll have to play it for me later."

"It's not finished."

"Just a few chords. I would love to hear it."

She looked down at the tips of her boots as red rushed into her cheeks. "Maybe. We'll see."

He gave her another quick kiss on the lips before he turned on his heels and headed for the door. "I'll be in the barn."

The doors banged against the wall in the dining room as he left.

He whistled softly as he made his way out to the big structure in the distance. He loved the smell of hay and horses. Something about the scents soothed his soul. Of course, being raised on a ranch probably had something to do with it.

The cooler temperature of the barn caressed his bare forearms as he stepped inside and grabbed the shovel from the corner to the left where they kept all the shovels, rakes, wheelbarrow, and so forth for cleaning the stalls. Country music from the radio played softly in the background. He recognized that voice. The song was Samantha's newest release called Country Boy. It was one of his favorites.

The hard physical labor would do him good, help get the testosterone out of his system from kissing Samantha. Damn, she had soft lips. He hadn't really had the chance to enjoy the one she bestowed on him when they were on stage together so this one was awesome in its own right. She definitely knew how to kiss.

As he took the wheelbarrow and shovel to the first stall, his thoughts drifted to what her experience with men might be. She seemed almost shy in some circumstances, but in others, she knew how to please a man. That wasn't something one typically asked a girl though. He wasn't stupid enough to bring up the subject with her either.

Scoop after scoop of horse shit made it into the wheelbarrow as he worked silently to rid himself of the boner he sported. The physical work didn't seem to be doing much since all he had to do was remember the feel of her lips on his and it came back with a vengeance.

"Jackson?"

"In here."

A moment later, the girl stood in the doorway of the stall he was working on. "Where's another shovel?"

"Near the door to the right as you are facing outside."

"Be right back."

"Are you sure you want to do this? Isn't it hard on your hands?"

"Like playing the guitar isn't? I have calluses on my calluses."

He laughed. "I guess so. I hadn't really thought about it, but yeah, guitar strings are hard on the fingers."

"Have you ever played?"

"I've dinked around some. I can play a little."

"I'll give you the sheet music for one of my songs. We can play together."

"I'm not good enough to play with you."

"Jackson, I'm self-taught on the guitar just enough to write. I don't play on stage for a reason. That's the band's job."

"Oh, right."

She stood with another shovel and wheelbarrow at the opening to the stall. "Where to, captain?"

"The stall next to this one needs to be done."

"I'm on it."

They worked in silence for several minutes before she said, "Jackson?"

"Yeah."

"How many women have you been with?"

*Oh, we are going there, are we?* "A few."

"Like how many?"

"Probably fifteen. Why?"

"I'm just wondering how experienced you are in comparison to me."

"How many guys have you been with?"

"Two."

"Really?"

"Yep. It's hard being on the road all the time. I never know who is around me to be with me or to latch onto the money they think is there."

"I can imagine."

"It's very frustrating."

They worked for a few more minutes. "Have you had a steady boyfriend at all?"

"In high school, but not since I started touring. I have to be so careful."

"I bet."

"How about you? Any girl broke your heart?"

"Nope. I've had a couple of girls I've been with for a few months, but never anyone seriously."

"I don't understand why. You are a cute guy, rugged, probably great in bed, very adventurous to be okay with going on the road with me, what's the problem?"

"I haven't found anyone I wanted to be around for a long period of time, I guess." He shrugged as he dug into the pile of manure in the stall.

"You do realize we will have sex before this is all said and done, right?"

"We will?"

"Yes."

"You're sure."

"Yep."

"How can you tell?"

"Because the kiss in the kitchen almost made me want to fuck you right there on the counter. Good thing we didn't. I'm sure Millie would have been completely embarrassed to find us in a precarious situation like that."

He could hear the shovel making contact with the ground as she worked. She never missed a beat, even with the sexy conversation they were having.

She knew they would have sex, huh? Good thing he was completely on board with the idea. He almost wished they could sneak up to the loft to fuck like bunnies right now, but he kind of wanted their first time to be in a bed with soft sheets and fluffy pillows. "I'm sure she's seen a lot of things over the years in the main lodge. After all, six out of nine of us are paired up. It's hard for some of them to get alone time anywhere on this place."

"I'm sure."

"Do you want to see a bit more of the barn?"

"Of course. It's a great structure. I don't think I've seen one this big in a long time. Is there a big loft?"

"Yep and it's seen a lot of action too."

"What hasn't on this ranch?"

He laughed. "Very true."

"I'm almost done with this stall. Are there shavings to put down?"

"Yeah. There is a huge pile outside to the right. The pile farther back is for the manure."

"Got it." She moved past him with the wheelbarrow as he finished the stall he'd been working on.

He'd been distracted. That had to be the reason she finished before he did or there was less shit in the stall she'd been working in. It couldn't be because she scooped the whole time they talked while he leaned on the handle of the shovel, right?

She returned to the barn as he was wheeling his own load outside. "I can do another one if you want? I'm sure there are tons more to do. You guys have a lot of horses."

"Sure, if you want or we can get back to it after we tour the barn."

"It's big, but I don't think it will take very long."

"It depends on how much you distract me."

"Me?"

"Yep. You are definitely a big distraction with those lips, that body, and those hands."

"My hands. How do you figure?"

"When you touch me, it makes everything go haywire."

"Oh, I like that. I'm glad I'm not alone then because you kind of make my body do some weird tingling things too."

"Oh yeah?"

"Yes, sir."

"I like the sound of that."

"Do you now?"

"Hmm. Let me get rid of this and we'll see where this goes when I get back."

"Hurry."

"I will."

He practically ran around the backside of the barn to dump the load of shit into the pile, load up his wheelbarrow with shavings and run back.

She hadn't moved, but the smile on her lips told him she knew exactly what she was doing to him as she teased him mercilessly with her body, lips, and eyes. *Lord, I want her bad.* A tight pair of jeans encased her long legs. She wore a little tank top with spaghetti straps across her shoulders, leaving them open for his mouth. The boots on her feet looked fairly new, although he knew she probably only had her dress boots to wear so they all were new. Her hair was back in a braid now, which she must have done after she finished the cookies to keep it out of her face while she shoveled.

He hope she wasn't cold wearing that skimpy little top, but he knew exactly how to warm her up. His fingers tingled with the need to touch her, run them through her hair, skim them over her body, and find each and every spot that made her sigh. "Put the shovel down for now. I want to show you the tack room."

She leaned the shovel on the wall to her right. "I love the smell of leather."

"Me too." He left his wheelbarrow and shovel near the next stall. "Come on. We'll see if no one is in there."

"Ever fucked in the tack room?"

"I haven't."

"Want to?"

"Samantha."

"What?"

"I kind of want our first time to be in a bed."

She gave him a quick kiss on the mouth. "Such a traditionalist. You are kind of an old fashioned guy, huh."

"Yeah, I would say so."

"I could give you a blow job."

His body went flush with excitement. "I wouldn't say no."

"All right, then." She grabbed his hand and started pulling him toward the doors. "Let's find the tack room."

"Which one?"

"There is more than one?"

"Yeah, let's see the one in the back of the barn first. It's usually free of traffic as long as Joshua isn't in there working on his saddles and stuff."

"We won't be disturbed?"

"I can't guarantee that."

"Sounds like fun."

They reversed direction toward the dim rear of the barn where a large door stood closed. Jackson worked the lock on the door before swinging it open. The scent of leather met his nose when he inhaled a deep breath. He got a hard-on just thinking about fucking her in the tack room. Maybe he would change his mind about it, but then again, he'd been in a constant state of hard since their kiss in the kitchen. If she went down on him? *Holy hell*. He would be in heaven and probably blow his load in record time.

When he walked inside and turned around, she pulled the door shut, and flipped the latch before she turned around to give him the sexiest smile he'd ever seen on a woman. She sauntered toward him as he backed up to find the stool sitting in the corner. With a toss of her braid, she moved in closer.

She parted her lips as she leaned in toward him. The clink of his belt buckle sounded loud in the quiet room. She slowly unzipped his jeans before grabbing his hard cock in her hand as she pulled him free. "Holy shit. You have a Prince Albert?"

"Yeah."

"Wow. I've never seen one. Can I touch it?" she asked, her hand hovering over the tip of his cock.

"Of course." He wanted her touching him any way he could get her. Hand, mouth, breasts, he didn't care and if she wanted to play with the ball in his cock, so be it. He'd love to have her tongue wrapped around the head right now, but her fascination with his piercing was doing it for him at the moment.

"Did it hurt when they pierced through there?"

"A little."

"How does it feel having sex?"

"You'll find out soon enough."

Her hand moved over his cockhead, drawing a deep moan from his mouth.

"You're a big guy."

"Thanks."

"But I think I can take you." She stroked his cock up and down. "I can't wait to see what your piercing feels like in my pussy."

"Me either." He wrapped his hand around the back of her head. "But right now, I want your mouth on me."

"My pleasure, cowboy." She dropped to her knees and slowly licked his cock like an ice cream cone. "We need these jeans off."

"Down, just down. In case I have to pull them up quickly."

"Whatever. I want access to those nuggets waiting for me below. I want to suck them, lick them, and roll them in my mouth."

"You are such a dirty girl for only having been with two guys." He shoved his jeans off his hip so they rested around his knees.

"They taught me a lot about pleasing a man."

"Thank God," he growled low in his throat as she took the head of his cock into her mouth.

She flicked the piercing with her tongue several times. "This is fun."

"Suck. God, please suck."

She went down on his cock, taking almost the whole thing in her mouth. The head of his dick bumped the back of her throat as she breathed through her nose to accommodate his size. He knew most women gagged, but she was good, very good. Her fingers caressed his balls, dragging a groan from deep in his throat as he leaned back against the wall.

While she worked his cock with her tongue and his balls with her fingers, he tried to put his mind on something, anything that would forestall the explosion of cum from his dick into her waiting mouth. Her movements tore his concentration to shreds in a matter of minutes.

"I'm going to come."

"Please do." She licked one side, then the other before working her mouth over the end of his cock again.

She wanted him to come in her mouth, he would accommodate her wishes. His balls drew up taut and aching toward his groin. A moan surfaced to his lips while he shot his load down her throat in long spurts of cum.

As his cock softened, she slowly licked him clean before stuffing him back in his pants. "Thank you."

"For what?"

"For the blow job. It was magnificent."

She smiled as one perfectly arched eyebrow rose over her right eye. "I'm glad you liked it."

A knock sounded on the door. "Jackson?" It was Jeff.

"Yeah?"

"I thought you were cleaning stalls?"

"We were. I'm showing Samantha the tack room."

"Uh, okay."

"Did you need something?"

"Nope. Carry on."

"Wow. Does that happen a lot?"

"Yeah. I told you this barn gets a lot of use."

"The tack room too?"

"Yes, ma'am. I'm sure we've all used this room a time or two over the years."

Her bottom lip stuck out in a pout. "You mean I'm not the first girl to blow you in the tack room?"

"Sorry, but no. You were the best though, so far."

Indignation rushed across her features, pulling the corners of her mouth down in a frown. "So far?"

"Well, you never know where we are going, Samantha. I can't say you'll be the last to have her way with me in the barn either, just like I can't say I'm the last guy who will fuck you in the bed on your bus."

Her mouth screwed up in a twisted kind of grin. "True."

"See."

"Okay. I'll forgive you for your words."

He rolled his eyes as he rebuckled his belt. "We should get back to work."

"Fuck and run. I see how you are."

"I told you. I want our first actual sex session to be in a bed. Mine, yours or otherwise wouldn't bother me."

She leaned in and brought their mouths together in a deep kiss. "I want you to fuck me every way you can think of."

"I want that too."

"It's a date. In my room later tonight?"

"I'll be there."

"Good." She kissed him again. "I can't wait."

"Me either."

# Chapter Seven

Blackness surrounded the cabin as Jackson made his way to the one Samantha was occupying with stealthy feet so he could keep their rendezvous secret from his family. He didn't want them all to know they were having sex, though they probably already figured as much.

The light burned in the window of her cabin when he stepped up on the porch to knock. She didn't give him the chance. The door flung open. She grabbed his hand and dragged him inside the room before slamming the door shut behind him. "I'm glad you're here," she said breathlessly. "I've been imagining this all afternoon."

"You too?"

"Yeah. Are you excited?" She glanced down at his straining cock. "I guess you are."

"I've been replaying our little rendezvous over and over in my mind since you sucked me off in the barn."

She grabbed for his belt. "I can't wait to get you out of these pants."

"You say the sexiest things."

He took ahold of her top at the edges near her stomach so he could lift it over her head and toss it to the side. He wanted to see her, all of her. When her breasts were free from the confines of her top, he stopped to admire the round globes with their dusky pink nipples. They were perfect, just like her. "Beautiful."

With both hands, he took the flesh in his palms and rubbed his fingers over her already hard nipples. She leaned into his touch, begging for more with her gaze. "Lick them."

"Oh, I plan to lick, suck, and anything else I can think of to do to them. Maybe even fuck them." He walked her backward until the backs of her knees hit the bed and she fell to the mattress. Her blonde hair encircled her head like a halo. He knew she was an angel when she sang, but man, he hadn't figured she'd fallen from heaven to torture him like this. He unbuttoned her jeans at the waist, and then pulled them along with her skimpy little thong, down her legs, leaving her naked on the bed. "You are gorgeous."

"Thanks, but I'd really like it if you wouldn't stare."

"I can't help looking at you. Realizing I'm going to get to make love to this beautiful woman has me almost dizzy with excitement."

"You're making me blush."

"Red looks good on you." He ran his hands from her feet, up her calves, and over her thighs until he reached the juncture where her treasures lie. "I'm going to eat you until you scream my name."

"Oh, God, yes." She spread her thighs laying everything open to his gaze.

Her pussy was magnificent as well. She didn't go completely bare but she only left a small thatch of hair on her pussy. The rest had been shaved clean. The pink petals of her labia glistened with juices, waiting for the first thrust of his hips. He needed to taste her first though. He'd been dreaming about this for a long time.

With both hands under her butt, he pulled her to the edge of the bed, went down on his knees, and breathed in her scent. Peaches and cream if he knew anything. She smelled wonderful. He couldn't wait to taste her.

Her hips bucked at the touch of his tongue against her outer lips. The moment he grazed her clit, she moaned, tossing her head from side to side, relishing in the sensations he gave her. He wanted to bombard her with everything he knew how to do. This was the ultimate test of his manhood. Could he please his perfect woman?

"Please."

He loved when she pleaded. The thought of her begging him several times to let her come, almost had him coming in his own pants before he had a chance to fuck her. That wouldn't do. He wanted to be inside her more than his next breath. The tip of his tongue touched her clit again, moving the little button of nerve endings back and forth until she almost sobbed in her need. Her hands clutched at the bed covering.

"God, Jackson. Please. Make me come. I'm dying here." He pushed two fingers into her pussy, bringing her hips off the bed. "Yes."

Her pussy grasped his fingers, sucking on the digits, trying desperately to keep them inside her. She was tight, so tight.

He could feel her quiver around his fingers as he continued his assault on her clit and finger fucking her until she exploded with her climax in a rush of liquid over his hand.

"Jackson!"

He brought her down slowly with soft licks and easy strokes. Her breathing slowed to almost normal.

"God, that was fantastic."

"I'm glad you enjoyed it."

"I can't wait for the rest."

He sat back on his haunches. "I have to ask. Are you on the pill?"

She leaned up on her elbows. "Yes. I take it for my periods even though I haven't been sexually active in quite a while."

"I'll still use a condom since we don't know each other very well."

"I haven't been with anyone in months."

"Me either, but I'd rather be safe than sorry later on for either of us."

"I'm okay with you going bare."

"I'm not. Not that I don't want to experience everything with you, but I'd feel better if I wore one."

"Whichever is good for you. I don't want to ruin the mood because, cowboy, I'm ready for you to be as deep as you can be."

"Hmm." He looked around the room debating on how he wanted to do this to make it good for her, missionary on the bed, modified cowgirl, anal? Of course he didn't know if she'd ever had anal before so that one was probably out for now, but he could get real creative from behind. "Okay, roll on your stomach."

Her eyes lit up as she bit her lip and slowly rolled onto her stomach. "What do you have in mind?"

"I'm going to take you from behind so I can play while I fuck you."

She glanced over her shoulder. "You could play anyway, cowboy. I like your hands on different body parts."

"Yeah, but this way I have your braid to hold onto."

"Ride 'em cowboy."

"Yee haw!"

She spread her legs, giving him a great view of her glistening pussy and her pert little asshole. He so wanted to take her there. Someday, he hoped to if they were together long enough. Up on his feet, he was a little tall to get to her readily, so he shoved two pillows under her hips to bring her assets a little closer to his height.

"There we go."

"Hurry. I'm dying here."

He scraped his finger through her folds before slowly penetrating her with two fingers. Damn, she was wet and ready for his cock. A shiver rolled through him at the sight of her juices on his fingers. Her taste had been like an aphrodisiac to his mouth when she'd come all over his face, now he wanted to see the same liquid coating his cock.

He grabbed for his pants on the floor beside him, reached into his wallet, and pulled out a condom. After he rolled the slippery latex down on his cock, he positioned himself at her opening and slowly pushed inside her. Man, she was tight. Obviously, she hadn't been with anyone in quite a while. It was like slipping his hand into a mink lined glove. Goose bumps broke out on his skin.

She wiggled her hips.

He gritted his teeth trying to hold back the orgasm hovering on the edges of his sanity. He couldn't come yet. *Train wrecks. Lots of train wrecks. Gory images should help me concentrate.*

"Jackson," she pleaded, pushing her cute little ass back, impaling her pussy further on his cock.

"Easy. You feel so fucking fantastic, I won't be able to hold back if you move."

She groaned as he slipped farther inside her. "God, that piercing feels awesome scraping along my vagina. Holy crap."

Once he managed to get his cock as deep as he could, he closed his eyes and bit his lip. Pain would keep him focused, right? It had to, otherwise he would blow his load in nothing flat. Her pussy felt so good, he couldn't stand the feelings bombarding his body.

He pulled back, and then shoved in again.

Her high-pitched moan bounced off the walls. "Fuck. Do that again."

The idea of hitting her G spot beckoned as he pulled out. Pushing in with a snap of his hips, he hit the elusive little spot behind her pelvic bone.

"Oh my God. What the hell did you hit with that ball? That's fantastic."

"Your G spot."

"Holy hell, that's fabulous. I've never had anyone hit it before." Her whole body broke out in one big shiver. "Keep it up, cowboy, and I'll be coming soon."

"Good because I don't know how long I can last. Your pussy feels amazing."

"Fuck me hard, Jackson. Give me everything you got."

He didn't need any more encouragement as he began rocking against her ass, shoving his cock so deep inside her. Within minutes, they were both hovering on the edges of climax. He grasped her braid in his hand and wrapped the hair around his fist so he could pull her head back.

"Hell yeah."

Their mutual climax broke over them like a wave breaking against a jetty's ragged rocks, throwing water against the peaks in a crashing sound loud enough to hurt your ears.

Cum trickled down between them as she squirted around his full cock. Her responsiveness didn't surprise him. She seemed the type to give everything to whatever she was doing at the time and having sex seemed to be no different.

As their bodies cooled and his cock softened, he leaned in to bite her on the shoulder, then sucked her delicate white skin into his mouth, leaving a small purple mark on her back. At least for now, she was his.

* * * *

She curled into his body like she'd been made to be there. His chest made a great pillow as she sifted her fingers through the hair curling around his nipples. The small ring on his right nipple tantalized her, so she flicked it with her fingernail.

"Having fun?"

"Yes. I've never been with a man who has piercings before."

"You don't mind them, do you?"

"Hell no!" She propped herself up on her elbow so she could look him in the face. "I think they are sexier than anything and the tat running from your shoulder to your forearm is cool. You are just a very surprising man, is all. I would never expect a downhome country boy like you to have piercings and tats." She ran her hand from nipple to nipple and then down his abdomen, tracing each ridge with her fingertips. When she curled her fingers around his cock, he started getting hard in her hand. "Again?"

"Sure."

"Maybe this time won't be quite so fast."

"Are you complaining? You had two orgasms that I counted, correct me if I'm wrong."

"I'm selfish. I want more of this magnificent body."

She scooted down on the bed to position herself between his legs. The piercing in his cock fascinated her as she ran her tongue around the ball on the tip. The smaller one on the underside of his cockhead slid along her tongue as she took the head of his cock in her mouth. Both balls together had felt fantastic inside her pussy. The one on the head scraped along her G spot while the other one rubbed along her vagina in the most amazing dance of pleasure her nerve endings had ever experienced. Anticipation of having him inside her again had her pussy soaking wet.

As she slowly slid her tongue up and down the length of his cock, she could make out the faint trace of leather on his skin from his time in the saddle today. God, it turned her on to have such a sexy scent on him. The smell just did something inside her whenever she had a chance to be around it for any length of time.

His deep moan brought her thoughts back to the man. He was perfect in every way. Strong, loyal, faithful, sexy, and about the best thing she'd ever had walk into her life. She wanted to keep him for a good long while, but convincing him to be her boy toy might be a little difficult since he was such a strong-minded individual. Money usually worked well in situations like this. Yeah, she'd offer him a sum he couldn't refuse to stay with her. They hadn't really worked out the details of him going on the road with her, but now that they were having sex, surely he would want to stay with her, right?

"You're killing me, darlin'."

"I'm trying, cowboy."

"You have such a sexy mouth."

"Glad you like it."

"Both here," he touched his lips, "and there." His hips pushed up toward her as he moaned deep in his chest.

She had him right where she wanted him, ready to beg for an orgasm. "Jackson?"

"Yeah?"

"You do have another condom, right?"

"Yes, in my pants."

"Thank God." She grabbed his jeans from the floor, pulled the condom out of the front right pocket, opened it with her teeth, and then slowly rolled it down his length.

By the time she had him gloved, he was groaning, pulling her up his chest. She straddled his hips and positioned his cock, so she could do a slow glide down its thick length.

"Ride me, cowgirl."

"My pleasure, babe."

By the time she had him fully inside her, she'd lost her train of thought. The damned little ball on the tip of his dick rubbed her special little spot so enticingly she couldn't hold back the moan escaping her lips. Bracing herself on his chest, Samantha leisurely moved up and down his cock and shivered from head to her toes. Each thrust of his hips drove the ball right against her spot, driving her absolutely crazy with need.

"You know what?"

"What?" she asked, her concentration ebbing and flowing with the thrust of his hips.

"You feel amazing."

"You do too."

He braced his feet on the bed, giving him more leverage to thrust his hips up, shoving his cock deeper than the time before. She felt like she was about to implode from everything bombarding her.

When he lowered his legs again, she leaned back with her hands on his thighs and thrust her pussy forward. The little ball changed positions inside her body, giving her a whole new myriad of sensations to handle. She whimpered with need. She wanted to come so badly, she ached with it.

"Jackson, please."

"Tell me what you want."

"I don't know. God, help me."

He had one hand on her right hip as the other reached down between her legs to rub her clit. After a minute, he sucked his finger into his mouth, wetting the callused surfaced just enough so it would slide over the hard little nub.

*Yes, that's it, right there.*

Desire tightened her abdomen as she continued to ride his cock, gyrating and wiggling until she got just the right angle. With his finger rubbing her clit, she exploded in a burst of desire so hot, she felt scorched from the inside out.

"Jackson!"

Cum spilled over his cock, wetting both of them.

"Wow, you're a wet one, lady."

Her breath came out in small little pants as she tried to bring her breathing back to normal. "You make me that way." His hips began a slow rhythm of thrusting. "Shit, you didn't come yet?"

"Nope."

"I'm sorry. Want to switch positions or something?"

"I'm good with this, but lean over my chest. I'll thrust from below."

"Okay." She splayed herself over his chest, burying her nose in his neck. He smelled good enough to eat.

He kneaded her ass with his hands as he slowly built his thrust to where he pounded into her body in a steady rhythm. Her own need began to build again as he rammed himself inside her, filling her to capacity. The fullness of having him there, made her feel whole.

When she climaxed again, it shocked her. It wasn't the explosive climax of earlier, but a small, pleasant experience as she milked his cock while he enjoyed his own orgasm. She didn't have to have a mind-blowing orgasm every time, right? The small ones were great in their own way.

As she lay on his chest, breathing in his scent, she realized she liked him...a lot, more than anyone she'd ever been with before. That was saying a whole bunch because she was around men all the time who wanted her attention.

Now she just had to figure out how to keep his attention, keep him in her bed and hogtie him to her life for a good long while.

"What was it you wanted to ask me before things got moving along in other directions?"

She sat up on his chest and leaned on her elbow. "Well, I was thinking. We hadn't discussed payment for you being on the road with me while we figure out who this stalker is."

"Payment?"

"Yeah. I mean you'll be riding with me on the bus, living with me basically, having sex with me on a regular basis I would guess, so we need to discuss payment."

"What the fuck?" He sat up to abruptly, she fell off to the side of him on the bed before he sprang to his feet, turning to face her. "You can seriously mean to pay me for my services?"

"Well, yeah. I mean I wouldn't expect you to do all it for free."

"Do you hear yourself?"

"What?"

"I'm not a fucking prostitute, Samantha."

"I didn't say you were."

"Well, you sure as hell are acting like I'm one wanting to pay me for services rendered. What? Are you going to start sticking dollar bills in my underwear now?"

"Seriously, Jackson, this is nuts."

"No it's not. I didn't make love to you so you could pay me. I don't need nor do I want your money."

"Everyone wants money."

"I have my own, thank you very much. I don't need yours."

"But I have way more than I could ever spend. I want to give you some."

He threw up his hands and dropped them to his sides in frustration. Carefully, he pulled the condom off his cock before tossing it into the trashcan near the bed.

"Where are you going?"

"Back to my room. Obviously, you have some weird sense of something, I'm not sure what. Entitlement maybe? Who the hell have you been hanging around anyway? If all of your so-called friends want money from you, you need new friends. Friends don't act like that and lovers don't want your money either unless that's all they're in it for. I'm not."

"What are you in this for, Jackson?" she asked, sitting up on the side of the bed. Hurt clouded her mind. She'd apparently done something wrong and she needed to figure out how to fix the situation.

"All I wanted was to spend time with you, get to know you. Samantha Harris the Iowa farm girl, not Samantha Harris the big country star."

"Don't go. I'm sorry. I didn't mean to insult you."

"You did."

"I said I'm sorry. What more do you want?"

"I think I need some space. I just don't want to be around you right now."

"Please, don't leave."

He shoved his legs into his jeans before throwing his T-shirt over his head. "I'm sorry, Sam."

She drew her legs up to her chest, holding in the hurt. She would cry when he walked out, but she wouldn't while he was there. Giving a man that kind of power over you was a bad thing, something she wouldn't think about right now. She wouldn't give him that power.

When he finally pulled open the door to leave, he glanced back over his shoulder. "I'll see you tomorrow. We can talk after I've had time to think."

"I'm sorry," she whispered, tears choking her words as the door slowly closed behind him.

# Chapter Eight

After spending a restless night flopping from one side of the bed to the other, Jackson finally got up at daybreak to start his chores. *Why the hell did she do that? Way to make me feel like a loser.*

He grabbed his jeans out of the dresser to slip them over his hips. Today should be an interesting day. He couldn't wait to see what Samantha came up with. She really had a weird sense of right or wrong. He shook his head before pulling a clean T-shirt over his head. By the time he'd stomped his feet into his boots, he was ready to face whatever the day brought, including Samantha Harris.

When he walked past her cabin, he hesitated, not sure whether he should try to talk to her this morning. He glanced at his watch. Six in the morning. Too early even though she was going to get up and do some chores with him, he figured he'd let her sleep. He'd catch her at breakfast maybe and see if they could work out the crazy thought process she had. Right now, he needed coffee.

As he approached the main lodge, the heavy wooden door opened and then closed without anyone going in or out. The ghost of the old cowboy was active this morning apparently.

Jackson pushed open the door and headed for the coffee urn to the left side. Luckily, someone was already up and had started it. He needed the fortification after his rough night.

Once he'd poured a cup, he doctored it with the normal offerings before heading into the main lodge area where the three big leather couches, tables, pool table and small gift shop sat. In here, a couple of weddings had taken place and many Christmases were celebrated, along with lots of birthday parties over the years.

He wandered outside to the front porch, taking a seat in the rocker to the right of the door. What the hell was he going to do about Samantha? Did she really think paying him was the way to get him to stay with her? Did she have no self-esteem or did she really think he was the type of guy she could pay off?

He sipped his coffee as rain began to drizzle off the roof. Great. What a shitty day this turned out to be.

For over two hours, he turned the situation with her over in his brain until his head began to hurt. *Maybe talking to Mom will shed some light on the subject, but then if I do that, she'll have to be in on the ruse.*

The door opened beside him, revealing the woman he thought hung the moon.

"Hey, son."

"Hey, Mom."

"You look lost in thought."

"I am kind of."

"Did you have a fight with Samantha?"

"Sort of."

"Do you want to talk about it?"

"If I do, I'm going to have to let you in on a secret."

"You know I can keep one if you need me to."

"I know." He set his empty coffee cup on the table next to his chair. "Sam and I aren't really a couple."

"Could have fooled me."

"I know and that was the plan. She has someone stalking her. She asked me to pretend to be her boyfriend for the next several months or until we can catch whoever is doing this."

"Okay." She took a drink of her own coffee. "I understand."

"Well, things kind of changed last night."

"Oh?"

"Yeah. We had sex."

"I would think it kind of means the ruse of a relationship is no longer a ruse."

"You know it takes more than sex to make a relationship."

"Very true. Do you think of your situation as a relationship?"

"I'm not sure."

"Tell me the rest. What did you fight over?"

"She basically wants to pay me for pretending to be her boyfriend, which includes us having sex on a regular basis."

"Hmm."

"Yeah. I totally feel like a prostitute here. She wants to pay me for sex."

"No. She wants to pay you for pretending to be her boyfriend."

"Which includes having sex."

"That's a benefit of the situation, I'm assuming."

"I'm sure it would be."

She took another sip of her coffee. "Think of it this way, Jackson. She's a young woman surrounded by people who want to be near her for whatever reason. They want her attention. They want her money. They want her fame. She doesn't know who to trust. She obviously trusts you to some extent, but she's not used to having someone do something for her just because they want to help. It is who you are."

"I do want to help her."

"Then make her understand that, honey. Having someone around without an agenda is new to her."

"Do you really think talking to her would fix the situation?"

"Yes."

The bell clanged for breakfast. They both stood and he leaned in to kiss his mom on the cheek. "Thanks, Mom. You always know what to say."

"I'm a listener. She's a complicated young lady, but one who, I think, will give you a good run for your money if you let her."

"Stop matchmaking. I don't want a long-term relationship with her. Helping her doesn't require that."

"You never know where things might lead, though, Jackson."

"I know, but I certainly am not looking for it right now."

"You should be. You aren't getting any younger, mister." She pushed her still coal black hair over her shoulder. "Neither am I."

"You look fabulous, Mom, and you know it. You don't look a day over thirty-five."

She pushed against his shoulder. "Get out. I certainly do not look thirty-five, forty-five maybe."

They laughed as he pushed open the door to the lodge to head in for breakfast. When they reached the dining room, he glanced around, but didn't see Samantha. *Oh well. Maybe she slept in this morning.* She certainly deserved some relaxation and he'd do everything he could do give it to her.

Plus, he had chores to do to keep him occupied today. They were bringing some of the cattle down from the north pasture to get them ready to take to market. It was their last run before spring. He could be riding herd all day even though they would be back in for lunch and then back out again afterward.

After breakfast, he managed to sneak a few leftover chocolate chip cookies before he headed to the barn to saddle his horse. The rain would put a hamper on their work, but rain or shine didn't matter, work needed to be done anyway.

He pulled his hat low on his forehead before dashing across the yard, dodging as many raindrops as he possibly could. His mad dash into the shaded interior of the barn stopped the moment he crossed through the double doorway. His horse stood in the stall three down from the end. The big bay gelding was his special friend. He'd owned the horse since he was twelve and bought it himself with the money he'd saved shoveling out stalls for the neighbors one summer. Hot, backbreaking work, but he was proud to say he owned one of the best cutting horses in the county.

"Hey, boy."

The horse knickered softly as Jackson approached to stroke his nose.

"We have a lot of work to do today." The horse nudged his shoulder. "Let me get your tack and we'll get a move on."

A few minutes later, found him mounting his horse, tapping him with his booted heels and making their way out of the barn. *Today is going to suck donkey balls if this rain doesn't stop.* He glanced back at Samantha's cabin, noting the curtains still pulled tightly shut and shrugged. She'd missed breakfast, but she probably had stuff on her bus she could eat if she got up between now and lunch. She's a big girl, he figured she could handle missing breakfast.

He met his brothers at the back of the corral where they all lined up to head out to the pasture. It would be a long day at this rate.

When he returned right before lunch, he noticed the curtains still drawn shut on Samantha's cabin. He wondered if she'd make an appearance for the noon meal. Maybe she was avoiding him after their blowup last night. She might still be pissed at him, although her face last night said she was more hurt than pissed. If she didn't show for lunch, he would get the spare key and check on her. He was getting a bit worried about her.

The bell clanged to signal lunch as he tied his horse to the hitching post inside the barn with some water and feed. The horse could rest out of the weather while he ate.

As the meal progressed without a sign of Samantha, the worry became more prominent. He hadn't left that late the night before.

*Everything is all right. It has to be.*

When the meal concluded and she never arrived, he found his mom in her office. "Mom, can I have the key to Samantha's cabin?"

"Why?"

"I haven't seen her all day. She hasn't taken any meals. She doesn't have a car to go anywhere else and I've already checked her bus. She's not there. I'm worried."

"Sure, baby." Nina grabbed the key off the board on the wall. "Let me know what's up."

He took the key in his hand and quickly headed through the lodge toward the door. Trepidation surrounded his heart. Something was wrong. He knew it in his gut. When he approached the door, he decided to knock first just to make sure she wasn't sulking her day away in her cabin after their fight.

"Samantha?" He knocked several times without an answer. He leaned his ear against the door. Was that a moan? "Samantha!" He shoved the key into the lock and turned it. He called her name again as he pushed open the door. Daylight spilled into the dark room, but he could see a figure under the blankets on the bed. "Samantha?"

He walked slowly toward the bed, fearing the worst. With the toe of his boot, he kicked something glass against the wall. The room stunk like alcohol.

"Samantha, wake up."

She moaned softly, but didn't arouse.

The sheet had pulled down over her breasts revealing she was at least naked on the top as her rosy nipples peeked out from the edge. He swallowed hard when his cock jumped to life at the sight.

He touched her arm. "Samantha, wake up," he said again, shaking her slightly.

She didn't even moan this time.

The light on the lamp flicked on with a twist of his fingers. An empty bottle of Jack Daniel's lay against the wall where he'd kicked it, with another half-empty bottle sitting on the nightstand.

"How much fucking whiskey did she drink? Holy shit!" He lifted her eyelid, peering at her pupils. They were dilated and the whites of her eyes were bloodshot red. Her breathing was deep and unlabored. He shook her hard enough to wake the dead as he called her name again. She didn't stir.

He pulled out his cell phone and called 911, giving them the address to the ranch, her condition, and an idea of how much she drank. "Hurry. She's unresponsive." After he hung up, he called his mother. "Mom, she's in bad shape. I don't know how much she had to drink, but she won't wake up at all. I've called an ambulance so they can check her out."

"Okay, honey. I hope she's all right."

"I don't know, Mom. This is serious."

"Sounds like it. Are you okay?"

"I'm fine, but I'll go to the hospital with her to give them her information and whatnot as best I can."

"I'll be out there in a second so you can go on her bus to find her information. Does she have a purse there?"

He glanced around the room. "Not that I can see. It might be on the bus."

"I'll be right there."

"Thanks, Mom." He hung up his cell and moved to the side of the bed to cover her naked body.

He didn't know what else to do to help her. This drinking thing would kill her if she didn't get help, but she wouldn't until something slapped her in the face to wake her up to the facts of life. Jacob had to go through the same thing. Maybe he could talk to Samantha and help her realize her destructive behavior would be the death of her. "Lady, I wish I knew what was causing you to do this so I could help you."

Jackson could hear the sirens coming up the street about the same time his mother appeared in the doorway of the cabin.

"It sounds like the ambulance is here."

"Yeah."

"You go find her purse."

"Thanks."

"I'll tell them all I can. Still no idea how much she had?"

"No, not really. There is an empty fifth on the floor by the wall that I kicked when I came in and another half-empty bottle on the table there."

"Wow," his mom whispered.

"I know."

"Does she normally drink like this?"

"I'm beginning to wonder. We'll talk more when I've had a chance to confront her about this, but I'm betting she's got a bit of an alcohol problem. Her behavior is very telling and reminds me a lot of Jacob before he met Paige."

"I hope we can help her."

"Me too." He walked to the door. "The ambulance is pulling up now. I'll go see if I can find her purse in the bus while they check her."

"Okay."

The paramedics hurried up the walkway with their gurney. "Where is the patient?"

"In her bed. My mother will give you the details we know. I'm going to find her personal information, if I can, so you have it."

"Thanks."

As they rushed inside to treat Samantha, Jackson ran toward the back where her bus sat parked. The door opened with ease as he pulled on the handle. *Best check her bedroom.* Yep, her purse was sitting on the bed. He grabbed it by the handles, but stopped for a moment as he thought about going through her personal things. It wasn't kosher to do that to someone. *She gave up the right to be indignant about it when she drank herself unconscious.* He opened her wallet and glanced at her driver's license with her birthdate and address. She was twenty-nine this past March, so almost thirty. He wouldn't have guessed. Her tall, willowy form was something people wished for with her long legs, lean torso, nice sized breasts and flat abdomen. Of course, he would guess she'd never had kids or anything and she probably worked out frequently to keep her shape.

Shaking his head, he shoved her wallet back into her purse. He walked down the stairs of the bus and out to the waiting ambulance just as they wheeled her out on the gurney.

"I'm coming with you guys."

"You'll have to follow since you aren't family. We can only take the patient in the ambulance."

"That's fine. I'll follow then. I have her purse with her personal information like her birthdate, age, address, and so forth."

"They'll need the information at the hospital. We are taking her into San Antonio to University Hospital."

"Great. I'll meet you there."

His stomach clenched when they loaded her into the ambulance. Worry furrowed his brow. He hoped she'd be okay. He didn't wish this kind of thing on her, but hopefully she would learn from this experience and lay off the alcohol.

Forty-five minutes later, the ambulance pulled into the emergency entrance of the hospital while he parked his truck off to the side, grabbed her purse and headed in through the double doors.

"Can I help you?"

"Yes, they just brought in my…um a friend of mine through emergency. You will need her information to register her. She's unresponsive."

"What's her name?"

"Samantha Harris."

The clerk's head jerked up at the mention of Samantha's name. "Okay."

"I have her purse here with her address and everything on it. I don't know whether she has insurance or anything like that."

The clerk clicked the mouse and began filling in Samantha's information into the computer as he read off everything he could find on her driver's license.

"Do you know her medical history?"

"No, ma'am."

"All right. Have a seat. The doctor will be out to talk to you when they have her stable."

"Thank you."

He pulled out his cell to call Jeff and have him take care of his gelding since he'd forgotten at the house. "Hey."

"How's Samantha?"

"I don't know yet. I just got here. Can you take care of Scout for me?"

"Already done, bro."

"Thanks."

"No problem. Hey, keep us updated when you hear something. She's a nice girl, but it sounds like she might have some issues."

"Yeah, I think so too. I just hope I can help her with them."

"Aren't you getting in a little deep, Jackson? You just met her."

"I know, but there is something about her that's special. I can't put my finger on it."

"Easy, cowboy. She's got a lot on her plate to be taking on."

"Thanks, brother."

"Anytime."

He hung up the phone, preparing to wait. He knew how hospitals worked, slow and slower. Waiting wasn't in his genes. Unfortunately, this was going to be a long wait and an even harder confrontation when the time came.

Over an hour later, the doctor came through the door. "Uh, is there anyone here with Samantha Harris?"

Jackson stood. "I am."

"Follow me so we can talk in private."

"No problem."

The doctor led him back through a locked door, down a long hall and into a curtained off exam room. Samantha lay on the bed clothed in a hospital gown to her neck, with a sheet to her waist. Wires and tubes stuck out everywhere. He could see the monitor above her head beeping in a steady rhythm. Her breathing seemed deep with a slight snore. Her long blonde hair framed her head in almost a halo, giving her an ethereal look.

"We can talk here. There isn't anything I'm going to tell you outside of general details."

"Okay."

"She drank too much alcohol and is bordering on the upper level of alcohol poisoning. Her blood alcohol level is toxic. We are giving her fluids to keep her hydrated, monitoring her blood sugar levels, vitamin levels, and alcohol levels. We have to make sure she doesn't have seizures. We might have to pump her stomach."

Jackson blew out a breath as he took off his hat and raked his fingers through his hair. "How does this happen?"

"She drank a lot in a short period of time. When was the last time you saw her?"

"Last night about eleven. She didn't come in for breakfast or lunch today. When I went to check on her, this is how I found her."

"Did she appear to have vomited?"

"I don't think so. I found her in bed, but there wasn't any on the bed or pillow."

"Good. We are always concerned about aspiration with this kind of thing."

"I guess you are going to put her in the hospital?"

"Yes, for a couple of days to get her alcohol level down. She won't be released until it's zero."

"Good. Can you get her some counseling?"

"Does she have a drinking problem?"

"I believe so."

"Without her consent, no. She has to ask for help."

"Damn."

"I'm sorry. I wish I could do more."

"How long will she be out?"

"It's hard to say. It depends on how much she regularly drinks. This is most likely caused by rapid ingestion rather than her drinking over a period of time."

"Thanks, Doc."

"My pleasure." The two men shook hands. "We will be moving her to a room in the next hour or so. You'll be allowed to stay with her in the room upstairs if you wish."

"Okay." He sighed. "She doesn't have family here."

"I know who she is. She's got a beautiful voice and is very talented. Too bad this is the result of a quick rise to fame, probably."

"Yeah, I think so too."

"I've heard of it a lot with people in the music industry. I hope she lets you help her. You seem like a great guy."

"Thanks. I hope she lets me in. Right now, I think she's still in denial." He set her purse on the edge of the bed. "I'm going to see if I can get in touch with her parents to let them know what's going on."

"Good idea." The doctor laid his hand on Jackson's shoulder. "I think you'd be good for her."

The doctor walked out as Jackson opened her purse to see if she had a cell phone with her parent's number in it. This wasn't going to be an easy task.

# Chapter Nine

"Samantha?"

"Hi, um, no. My name is Jackson Young. I'm a friend of your daughter's."

"Where's Samantha, and why are you calling from her cell phone?"

"Is this her dad?"

"Yes, this is Michael Harris."

"I'm currently at University Hospital in San Antonio with Samantha."

"What? What happened?"

"I'm not exactly sure, sir. I was with Samantha last night. We had a little fight. I left her in her room at my family's ranch to go to bed. When I checked on her this afternoon, she was unresponsive in her bed. She was breathing and everything, but she wouldn't wake up."

"Holy hell. Is she going to be okay?"

"I believe so. She's in the emergency room right now. They're giving her fluids, monitoring her. She'll be here for a couple of days to flush the alcohol out of her system."

"Wait, alcohol?"

"Yes, sir. It appears she drank a lot of whiskey in a very short period of time last night or early this morning. The doctors are saying she's got alcohol poisoning."

"Oh my God. I told her to stop with the drinking or she would hurt herself, but she wouldn't listen. She's stubborn like that."

"I can imagine, sir."

"Who did you say you were again, son?"

"My name is Jackson Young. My brother's fiancé is the one who booked her to play the benefit concert in Bandera the other night. She's been staying at my family's guest ranch for the last couple of days."

"Oh yes. She mentioned you when I talked to her yesterday for a short time. Said you two were dating."

"Yes, sir."

"My wife and I will book a flight out tomorrow morning for San Antonio so we can be there to bring her home. She'll need to get some help with this problem."

"I understand, sir, but I don't think she'll go. She doesn't believe she has a problem."

"Well, son, with this episode, I think she does."

"I'm right there with you, but she won't get help until she comes to terms with it being a problem. Trust me on this. I had a brother who went through the same thing."

"She needs to be home with her family so we can take care of her."

"I'm sorry, sir, but I don't agree with you."

"I don't care what you agree with, young man. Her mother and I believe she needs to be in Iowa."

"What kind of treatment facilities are there for her? She probably needs inpatient treatment."

"We live in a small town. There isn't much here except corn and farms."

"I understand that, sir, but there is a top of the line treatment facility here in Texas where she can get the best treatment there is, if she'll allow it. Convincing her is the first step. She needs a firm hand, not someone who will buckle under her batting her eyes and giving you a little pouty lip."

"Are you saying we aren't hard enough on her?"

"Maybe. I don't know you and your wife or your family. I don't know Samantha that well, but we are trying to get to know each other in this weird little situation. I think she needs someone a little farther removed from her than family to be tough with her."

"What do you suggest we do?"

"Stay in Iowa. I'll keep her at the ranch with me and try to get her help here. She doesn't have to be on the road for a little bit longer so I'm hoping I can convince her to talk to someone at least."

"All right. Make sure to have her call us as soon as she is able."

"Of course."

"Thank you for calling, Jackson. You sound like a good guy. I hope you and Samantha become better acquainted. I think you'll be good for her."

"You're welcome, sir, and I hope to get to talk to you under better circumstances sometime soon."

"Take care of our girl."

"I will."

He hung up the phone and went to sit beside her bed. He brushed the hair back off her forehead and leaned in to kiss her there. She was something special, but damn if he knew what to do with her now. If she reacted this way every time they had a fight, he wasn't sure he could handle being with her even on a temporary basis. If he could get her off the alcohol and sober her up, she would be a handful he could really get into having with him daily. He took the chair next to the bed to watch her sleep.

They transferred her to a room upstairs about thirty minutes later, but she didn't stir much at all except to moan when they shifted her from the gurney to the regular bed in her room. Jackson got comfortable in the chair close by. It would be a long night at this rate.

About two hours later, she rolled her head toward him and cracked her eyes open slightly.

"Where am I?"

"At the hospital."

"Jackson?"

"Yeah."

She licked her dry lips. "What am I doing at the hospital?" She lifted her hand to her head. "Oh my God, I have such a headache. I feel like I've been kicked by a mule."

"I found you unresponsive in your bed at the ranch about three hours ago after you didn't come out for breakfast or lunch."

"What time is it?"

He glanced at his watch. "About five o'clock in the evening."

"What day?"

"You don't even know what day it is?"

She turned away from him. "No."

"We fought last night in your cabin so it's Monday."

"Shit," she whispered, turning back to face him. "I'm sorry."

"Do you want to tell me what's going on?"

"Nothing really."

He shoved his hands through his hair, wanting to do nothing more than pull it from his scalp in frustration. She didn't get it, apparently. "Nothing? I find you passed out in your bed with one completely empty bottle of whiskey on the floor and another half empty on your nightstand. The doctors are saying you had alcohol poisoning. You don't get that from leisurely drinking, Samantha. You get that from binge drinking. I've been reading up on it since you've been out cold, plus I dealt with this a lot with my brother."

"I'm sorry." Tears choked her words.

"Sorry isn't enough. You need help."

"I know."

"You know?" It would be incredible if she made things that easy to convince her, but he didn't think so.

She sat up farther in the bed, holding out a hand toward him. "I'll stop. I promise. No more alcohol. That's it. I'm done."

"I've heard those words before." He didn't believe her. This was the same trick Jacob had pulled when he'd confronted him on several occasions about his drinking. He hadn't binged on alcohol, but he'd drank until he was too drunk to walk many times. The night Paige had found him, he'd been so drunk, he'd puked in the hall at the Dusty Boot.

"Not from me."

"No, from my brother who didn't stop until he'd gotten his ass kicked in a bar fight and had to be rescued by a woman."

"I swear. I'll stop. It shouldn't be that hard, right? I mean I don't drink a lot normally."

"You were drunk when you came to breakfast yesterday."

"No I wasn't." Her hand shook as she held it out for him to take. "All right, yes, I'd had a few before I came to breakfast. It helps me when I'm writing songs. I makes the creative juices flow better from my brain to the paper, but I wasn't drunk."

"I could smell it on your breath."

"I know. I'd had a few, but I wasn't drunk."

"Did you have trouble walking? Were you having trouble concentrating on getting into the building?"

"I was a little wobbly."

He gave her an incredulous look. She really didn't believe she wasn't drunk and he couldn't fathom that. If she couldn't walk a straight line and had trouble with the smallest of tasks, yeah, she was probably well on her way to being three sheets to the wind.

"But I don't drink that much, Jackson, just a few to calm my nerves."

"Calming your nerves had nothing to do with last night. Did you get drunk because we fought?"

"You walked out on me."

"You practically called me a prostitute, Samantha. You offered to pay me for my services."

"I didn't mean for it to sound like I was paying you for your services. You jumped to the wrong conclusion. All I meant was to pay you for being my bodyguard and helping me catch this stalker." She nervously folded the sheet around her abdomen. "I never meant to insult you."

"Well you did, but my mother kind of made me see where you were coming from. It just didn't sound right the way you put it." He picked up her hand from where it lay on the white sheet. "I'm sorry I jumped to conclusions."

"I'm sorry I made it sound like I expected you to sell yourself to me."

He leaned in a kissed her on the lips. "How about we put this all behind us?"

"Sounds good. Can we start over?"

"Kind of hard to do since we've already had sex, but I'm game."

"Me too."

He looked over her face. She was pale and drawn. Her skin looked kind of sallow, too, and he expected it was all from the alcohol she drank. Her liver was still trying to process everything though. "I'm sorry I didn't ask this before. How are you feeling?"

"Like shit. Hung over would be a good term."

"I can imagine."

She glanced at the bag of fluid hanging from the pole next to the bed. "What are they giving me?"

"Fluids to help flush out the alcohol from your system faster. You'll be here until at least tomorrow. They won't let you go until your blood alcohol level is zero."

She exhaled as she closed her eyes. A tear escaped from the corner.

He felt like shit watching her cry, but he wasn't sure what to do. She needed to talk to someone and he didn't think he was qualified to deal with whatever stuff caused her to drink like she did.

"I think you need to talk to someone."

"Maybe."

"Jacob might be able to help or even Peyton. She's almost done with her degree in counseling and she's been in some tough situations before herself."

She wiped the errant tear from her cheek. "I could talk to them, I suppose, but I really don't believe I'm an alcoholic, Jackson. I can quit anytime I want to."

"I'm here to help you any way I can."

"And I appreciate that you are willing to do that."

The nurse came in a few minutes later. "My name is Camille. I'm the nurse who will be taking care of you for a few more hours. We change shift at seven. How are you feeling?"

"Like shit. Can I get something for a headache?"

"I'm sorry, but I can't even give you Tylenol because your liver is trying to process the alcohol in your system. You did a pretty good number on your body. Is there something you need to talk to a counselor about?"

"No."

"I have to ask this now that you are awake and aware. Were you trying to hurt yourself in any way?"

"Hell no! I wasn't trying to kill myself. Are you nuts?"

"Sorry. I had to ask with the way you came into the emergency room."

"What a thing to ask someone."

"It's protocol." She checked the needle in Samantha's arm, took her temperature, blood pressure before checking her heart and lungs. "Everything looks good. We will be drawing blood quite frequently during the night to check your levels and make sure your liver is functioning well."

The woman glanced at him, lowered her eyes, and smiled like she was flirting with him right in front of Samantha. *Wow*. The whole scene took him aback.

"Will you being staying the night with your girlfriend?"

He wanted to tell the nurse Samantha wasn't his girlfriend, but he figured if they were trying to pull off this ruse, he'd better play the part. "I can't. I have to work."

She smiled again. "We'll make her as comfortable as possible." The woman licked her lips before tilting her head to the side. "Are you a real cowboy?"

"As real as they get, I reckon. I live on a ranch with my family out in Bandera."

"Very nice." Camille gave him a once over from the top of his cowboy hat to his duty boots.

Thinking he could discourage the woman, he pulled Samantha's hand to his mouth and kissed her fingers. "We'll go shopping for a ring after you get out of here. Okay, babe?"

"Really? Wow. I love you, Jackson."

"I love you too, Sam."

The nurse frowned and took a couple of steps back. "Uh, I'll check on you later."

"Thank you."

As soon as the door closed behind her, Samantha pulled her hand from Jackson's grasp. "It wasn't just me, right? She was ready to jump you right here in front of me."

"Yeah, I think so."

"Does that happen often?"

"Not as much as you apparently think."

"You're a good looking guy. I would think it happens a lot."

"Nope."

Samantha laughed. "You're just being shy."

"Not really." He shrugged as he tugged at the thighs of his jeans to pull them down a bit. "My brothers get more attention than I do, especially the triplets. I think they've even been propositioned for a threesome."

"Now that I could believe."

"What is it with you women and sharing? I don't share."

"A little possessive are you?"

"A lot possessive of the woman I'm in love with, other than that, not so much."

"You would let a woman you were dating, date someone else at the same time?"

"I didn't say that, but if she was really into wanting sex with two guys..." He shrugged, letting the sentence die.

She sat farther up in the bed. Apparently, the thought intrigued her. "Really? You'd do a ménage?"

"As long as I didn't have to have sex with the other guy, sure. Why not?" He pointed a finger at her. "But not if we are in a serious relationship. If we were casually dating, then there wouldn't be any feelings involved."

"Oh, so you're saying if you love her, then you won't share, but if you don't, all bets are off."

He gave her a one-shoulder shrug. "Sure, I guess, although I haven't been faced with the situation, so I'm not sure how I would react to tell you the truth."

"What if I said I wanted you and Joey?"

His heart thumped loudly in his chest. Joey was his brother. Could he share a woman with him? Could he share Samantha with him? "I don't think that would be a good idea."

"What if it was a guy you'd never met?"

He still didn't like the way his gut clenched at the thought of watching Samantha with another guy. Not that they were exclusive or anything, but for now, she belonged to him. Nope, he decided he wouldn't share well.

"No."

"So you have a little double standard there?"

"Not really." He got to his feet and moved toward the window. He didn't like where this conversation was heading at all. She didn't need to be dating or having sex with anyone but him. *What if she really wanted to though? It's not like we are really a couple or anything, right?*

"I think you do, Jackson. What if I said I wanted a ménage?"

"Without me?"

"With or without. It depends on if you are game or not?"

He spun around on his boot heels so quick, the room spun. "Who else are you having sex with?"

"I'm not. It's hypothetical, cowboy. Get your jeans out of your ass." She raised her hand and held it out to him. "I'm not having sex with anyone else. I don't want to. You brought up the question, not me."

He moved closer to take her palm in his. "Good. I don't like the thought of sharing you with anyone else."

"A little contradictory there?"

"Maybe. I can't see me sharing you."

"Good. I don't want to share either."

"You don't?"

"No. If you were to ask to bring another woman into the mix, I'd turn you down flat and that would be the end of any kind of relationship."

"Are we in a relationship?" he asked, taking the chair again as he continued to cradle her hand in his.

"Sort of, I guess. For what it's worth."

"Then we are discussing your drinking, for what it's worth."

She sighed heavily as she titled her head back against the pillow. "I do not have a drinking problem, Jackson."

"I believe you do."

"I told you. I'm quitting. I won't drink again unless it's casually and with you around. Okay?"

He didn't really believe her, but what else could he do? Until she realized she had a problem, he couldn't help her. He needed help with this. He needed his family's support behind him when he went through her bus and found her stash of alcohol because he had a gut feeling there was one there. Otherwise, how had she retrieved two bottles of Jack to drink last night?

"Where did you get the Jack Daniel's you drank last night?"

"I had it on my bus."

"Do you always carry such a large quantity of alcohol on the bus?"

"Sometimes. It depends on how far between gigs we will be traveling. I told you. I drink before shows to calm my nerves, but not that much. Maybe three or four glasses."

"Three or four?"

"Yeah, but they aren't full glasses. They are tumblers."

"Straight whiskey?"

"I put a little ice in it, but yeah, usually straight."

He coughed. *Holy shit!*

"What do you drink when you drink?"

"A couple of beers."

"Beer doesn't do anything for me. I don't like the taste."

He leaned back in the chair, folding his arms across his chest. This conversation just got real. "Yeah, I guess it wouldn't."

"What's that supposed to mean?"

"Samantha, three or four glasses of whiskey straight is a lot of alcohol. When did you start drinking?"

"When I was in high school, but only on weekends at parties and stuff."

"You've been drinking like this for twelve years or so?"

She laughed. "No, silly. I used to drink wine back then. Nothing strong. I started drinking whiskey when I got my record deal."

"Did you used to have to drink when you sang karaoke?"

"No, I was singing in front of friends mostly, so it didn't bother me. They'd already heard me sing lots of times. When I had to start singing in front of hundreds or thousands of people, I couldn't get the words out. The first couple of concerts were terrible. I sounded really bad. In fact, they made me lip-sync for a few shows. After that, I drank a little and things got better."

"Do you hear yourself?"

"What?"

"You are drinking at every show and from what I've seen while you've been on the ranch, you are drinking daily."

Her brow wrinkled as a frown pulled down the edges of her lips. "No. I don't think so."

"I do."

She shook her head. "It doesn't matter. I told you I would stop, and I will. I'm done with it. I'll figure out some other way to deal with my anxiety about getting in front of people to perform."

"Good."

"You do realize we need to hit the road like next week, right?"

"Next week?"

"Yeah. My next show is in California and it will take a bit to get there. I need to text the band and Mark to get them ready to roll."

"You have two buses, right?"

"Yeah. One for the band and one for me."

"Good. I really didn't want to explain my existence to them right away when most of them haven't seen me before the other day at the show."

"No worries. I'll take care of it."

"Is there anyone in the band or road crew that you feel could be the stalker?"

She bit her lip as she stared straight into his gaze. Her blue eyes were serious with the change of subject matter. He could tell she was really frightened by the thought of someone so close being the person who wanted to get to her.

"I don't think so, but it's hard to tell. Most of the guys have been with me for a long time, but we do switch our roadies frequently. We take on new people at each stop for security and whatnot." He could see her body shudder. She really was terrified. "What if we never find him or her?"

"We will."

"What if we don't? I will have to watch my back forever. I don't think I can do that, Jackson."

"I'll be there to protect you for however long you need me to."

She swung her legs around in the bed so she was sitting on the side with her knees between his. "I could really fall in love with you very easily, you know that? You are one special guy."

# Chapter Ten

The next day, Samantha waited for Jackson to pick her up from the hospital to bring her back to the ranch. The nurses had already removed the needle from her arm and she'd sat in her hospital gown waiting from him to bring her clothes since she was naked when they brought her into emergency room. She felt like a kid waiting for her parent. Was that what he was turning into, her father?

*Ewww.* That thought disgusted her. She didn't need another parent. Hers had been strict enough on her and her sisters growing up. She held out her hand, watching as tremors made it shake uncontrollably. Her head pounded as her stomach rolled. Sweat poured down her back. God, she hoped this wouldn't last long. Quitting the booze wasn't going to be as easy as she thought it would when she told Jackson she was done.

She licked her parched lips. A little sip would calm her if only she had the flask she kept in her purse handy. She stood to walk to the long, thin closet tucked into the wall to see if her purse might be in there. *The flask should be in hidden inside.* One sip wouldn't hurt anything. She opened the door, grabbed her purse, and moved back to sit on the side of the bed. The gown bunched up around her butt, leaving it exposed to the air in the room. Disgusted by the feel of the bare sheet on her ass, she stood, yanked the offending garment around her butt, and sat back down. "Stupid things."

With her purse in her lap, she opened the zipper and began to dig around in the contents. Wallet. Keys. Checkbook. Makeup. Pens. Notebook. She flipped through the contents one piece at a time. *Surely my flask is in here.* After she had everything on the bed, she smiled as she finally pulled out the silver flask with the small plastic top. *One sip, that's all I need.* She unscrewed the cap and tipped the flask to her lips.

The door to the room opened, surprising her. Jackson strolled inside with a large bouquet of flowers in his hands. "What the hell are you doing?"

She hid the flask behind her back. "Nothing."

He tossed the flowers on the bed, grabbed the flask from her hand, took it to the sink, and dumped the small amount of contents down the drain.

"That's mine!"

"Not anymore. You said you quit, remember?"

"I just needed a sip, Jackson. I'm so shaky. I have a terrible headache, and I'm really thirsty."

He tossed the empty flask to her. "Drink water."

"One sip wouldn't hurt."

"Yes, it will. You said you could quit anytime."

"I can."

"We'll see. No more, Samantha. That's it. If I catch you with anymore, I won't stick around."

"But I need you."

"No, you think you need the booze." He tossed her clothes on the bed. "Get dressed. We are going back to the ranch and you are going to talk to Jacob and Peyton." He cupped her face with his palms as he looked deep into her eyes. "Honey, I'm trying to help you."

"You aren't helping me by taking it away like this."

"Yes I am." He stepped back. "You need to see a doctor. I think there is medication they can give you to help you through the withdrawal symptoms. Jacob took something right after he quit."

"I don't need medicine to help me. I can do this. I promise, I can do this."

"You can't do it alone, and yes, you do need the medicine. It's not good for you to go cold turkey as you can see by your symptoms."

A lump formed in her throat, forcing her to swallow hard. "I'm sorry. I thought one little sip wouldn't hurt me and it would help me get through this."

"It's okay, darlin'. We'll do this together."

"You are so good for me."

"My family will help too. We've been through some rough things as a group."

"I don't want them to know."

"They already do. I couldn't help but tell them what was going on when they took you away in an ambulance the other day."

"Well shit."

"It'll be okay. We tend to gather people to us when there is trouble, and baby, you are full of trouble right now."

"Thanks, cowboy."

He smiled as he brushed the hair back from her forehead. "You're welcome. Anytime, darlin'." He picked up the clothes and handed them to her gently. "I'll let you get dressed. I think the nurse was waiting for me to show up to boot your ass out of here."

"Yeah. She's already given me discharge papers."

"Okay. I'll step out."

She raked her gaze from the top of his head to his feet. "Not like you haven't seen it all before." He flushed red and she had to giggle a little. "Did I embarrass you?"

"Just get dressed. I'll be out in the hall."

She shook her head as she stripped off the gown. The pink lacy bra sitting on the bed gave her pause. She wondered if he picked it out himself or he had his mother grab her some clothes from her suitcases in the cabin. Probably his mom, she figured. Not that they hadn't already been intimate, but she thought it kind of funny how flustered he got with the threat of seeing her naked. Surely they would be doing the horizontal mambo again soon. She certainly wanted to experience the nice little ball he carried around on the end of his dick. It sure had felt good.

After she finally got dressed, she grabbed her purse, stuffed everything back inside, and then opened the door to find him leaning against the wall nearby. He sure was one sexy-ass man, she had to admit. She was really glad they were a couple, well sort of. Their relationship had a weird bit of a twist to it.

"Ready?"

"Yeah."

The nurse arrived with a wheelchair. "Sit, please."

"I can walk." She eyed the wheelchair with disgust. There wasn't any reason why she couldn't walk down to his truck.

The nurse pointed to the chair, indicating Samantha needed to sit. "It's protocol. We have to take you down in a wheelchair for your own safety." She glanced at Jackson. "Where are you parked?"

"Out front."

"You can go down and pull around to the loading zone near the doors. We'll follow you down."

"All right." He headed down the hall with them following close behind.

Samantha sniffed the flowers in her hands. They really were beautiful. She couldn't believe he'd actually bought her flowers. Guys didn't do this kind of thing anymore, did they? Well, he apparently did. She kind of got the feeling he was one of those gentlemanly types who liked to hold your door, give you flowers or give you their coat when you were cold. *His ass looks mighty nice in those jeans too.*

He really was the down to earth kind of man she'd always wanted when she thought of settling down. She wasn't sure he'd be the type to settle down with her though.

\* \* \* \*

The trip back to the ranch was made in silence. He wondered what she thought the whole time they drove, but he didn't want to ask. Hopefully, she was thinking about how she was going to quit the alcohol because she needed to.

His thoughts turned to when he'd walked into the room and found her about to drink from the flask. He didn't know what she was going for, but he knew he had to stop her. One sip would set her back days in her recovery.

He glanced at her hands clasped in her lap. He could see the trembling from his side of the truck. This wasn't going to be easy, he knew, but he was determined to help her get through this.

As they pulled through the gates of Thunder Ridge, she sighed.

"You okay?"

"Yeah."

"What's wrong?"

"This is going to be tough facing your family. I wish you hadn't told them."

"I didn't have a choice."

"I'm surprised it hasn't hit the tabloids yet."

"Uh, it has."

"Shit." She grabbed her purse and pulled out her cell phone. "The battery is dead."

"I'm not surprised."

"My manager is probably freaking out."

"He's called the ranch, but due to privacy issues, we couldn't tell him anything."

She rolled her head around on her shoulders like she was trying to pop her neck. "I'll call him as soon as I can plug this thing in. He'll need to issue a statement to the press."

"I think he already has according to the papers. He protected your privacy though and didn't tell them anything other than you were in the hospital being treated for an unknown ailment and would be discharged soon."

"That's good."

"Yeah. We haven't had the press out here yet. I don't think they knew you were staying with us."

"No, we kept that on the down-low."

"Good."

When they pulled up to the parking spaces, she glanced at the little cabin she called home for now. She wondered if Jackson would be joining her later this evening for a little fun or not. *Maybe not. My head is pounding and I feel like shit.*

"I already have it set up for you to talk to Jacob and Peyton."

"Now?"

"Yes. The sooner the better. I've also arranged for the doctor Jacob saw to make a house call. He'll be here in an hour to talk to you and get you some medicine."

"I guess."

"You have to start right away, Samantha. You can't do this alone."

"I know. I'm not feeling up to talking to anyone right now, but I'll do it for you."

"Do it for yourself, not for me."

"Okay."

He stepped out of the truck and moved around to her side to open her door. "Let's drop the flowers in your room before we head to the lodge."

"I have to do this talk at the lodge?"

"Yeah. Someplace open would be best for everyone involved. Jacob and Peyton will talk to you together."

"Great. Way to gang up on me."

"You'll see. It'll be fine."

Once they put the flowers in her cabin, he strolled back across the yard with her, cradling her hand in his. He knew this wouldn't be easy for her, but she had to start right now. Jacob and Peyton sat at one of the long tables as they walked into the large room. The rest of the place was empty, thank goodness. He didn't think she would do this if there were anyone else around.

"Peyton, Jacob, you both know Samantha."

"Hi Samantha. It's nice to see you again," Peyton replied. "Sit down. We don't bite."

"Hi. I'm not sure you remember me from the large gathering at breakfast the other day. I'm Jacob."

"Yes, I remember you and you as well, Peyton. Thank you for talking with me tonight and taking time away from your families."

"As long as you are with Jackson, you are family," Jacob replied. "Please, sit."

"Let's get started, shall we?" Peyton asked. "Are you staying, Jackson?"

"If Samantha wants me to."

"Yes!" She grabbed at his hand, drawing him down on the bench with her.

"I'll stay then."

Peyton drew out a pad of paper to jot some notes down on. "Why don't you tell us when you first started drinking?"

"In high school. I used to drink at parties."

"Do you know why you started drinking so early?"

"I wanted to fit in. Everyone drank."

She squeezed his hand like a lifeline.

"You can do this."

"Let me tell you a bit about myself, Samantha." Peyton set the pen down on the pad. "I was in an abusive relationship with an ex of mine. He physically, emotionally, and sexually abused me for years. When I finally decided I'd had enough, I took what I could before moving here hoping to stay hidden. I work as a bartender at the Dusty Boot so I see this kind of alcohol abuse all the time." She glanced at Jacob and smiled. "I used to watch Jacob come in time after time and get shitfaced although I didn't know the reasons behind it, I wanted to help. Fortunately, Paige found him, helped him, and he's been clean for a while now."

"But staying away from the alcohol is a never ending process. Most people, not all, but most people can't drink casually without going back into the same binge drinking that you and I suffer from." Jacob steepled his hands in front of his face as he regarded Samantha from across the table.

"Samantha thinks she can stop cold turkey." Jackson leaned in a kissed her on the head. "I've told her about the medication you took, Jacob, that helped with the symptoms of withdrawal."

"Yeah. The doctor will be here in a little while to help you with those things, but you have to take them regularly." Jacob picked up Samantha's hand, holding it between his. "You have tremors. I can feel them in your hand. I bet you have a headache, feel nauseated, and are anxious too."

"Yes."

"These are all symptoms of withdrawal." Jacob laid her hand back down. "How long have you been drinking heavily?"

"What do you mean by heavily?"

"Jackson said you drank an entire bottle of whiskey and half of another the other night. That's heavy drinking."

"I drink some before I go on stage."

"How much?"

"Three or four glasses. Straight."

Jacob didn't bat an eyelash, making Jackson wonder how much his brother had really drank over the years.

"I understand. I really do. Let me tell you a bit about my situation. I got a girl pregnant a few years ago. I knew about the baby. I asked her to marry me. She refused. She talked about abortion. I begged her not to. She did it anyway without my knowledge until a few days later when she told me. The guilt killed me. She killed my child and it wasn't something I could get over easily. I started drinking heavily. I was drunk at work, drunk at home, drunk at the bar, and driving drunk. I was lucky. I never hurt anyone, but one night I got into a huge bar fight with three big, burly guys over a pool game. I was betting and losing. They didn't want to take my money anymore and were prepared to walk away. I got in one guy's face. He hit me hard enough to scoot me across the floor on my ass. Paige stepped between us to save me. She's trained in martial arts so it wasn't much to her to protect me, but she did. When I remembered what happened later, I was so embarrassed by what she'd done, I quit drinking cold turkey."

"Did you go through withdrawals?"

"You could say that. It was bad. I basically stayed in bed for three days solid, not eating, not drinking, just shaking, vomiting, and so on."

"Wow."

"Yeah. I didn't see anyone but my mom for those three days. She finally got the same doctor who is coming out today, to come out here for me. He prescribed me some medication to help, but you can't drink with them. There are a lot of things you need to watch for. Seizures is one. DT's can kill you. They don't suggest you go cold turkey, but you can have the same symptoms and everything even if you just cut down dramatically from what you were drinking before."

"Basically, what Jackson wants us to do for you is to make you realize you aren't alone in this. We've both been in situations where we needed something.

The abuse I suffered through made me want to end my life on several occasions."

"I don't want to kill myself. I have too much to live for."

"Great, but you must realize you need to seek counseling with a professional substance abuse counselor."

"I thought you were."

"I'm in school for it, but I'm not done yet. You need to talk to someone who is experienced although I would love to talk to you anytime you want to. I'm sure Jacob would too."

"Of course I would. I'll be your sponsor if you want."

"I'd like that."

Jacob asked for a piece of paper from Peyton. "Here is my cell number. You call me anytime, day or night. I'll warn Paige so she won't freak when there is a phone call at three in the morning."

"I won't call at three."

"If you need me, you call. I don't care what time it is or where you are. If you feel like you are going to drink because you are depressed, anxious or whatever, you call me. Right, Jackson? I know he will be traveling with you in the coming weeks, but you call me if you need me."

A tear slid down her cheek. "I don't know how to thank you." She leaned into Jackson's embrace. "All of you. You've been so good to me and I've only know you people a few days."

"We care about you."

She shook her head as she wiped the tears from her face. "Thank you," she whispered.

He kissed the top of her head, holding her close while Peyton and Jacob stood. "Anytime, Samantha."

The doctor came through the door a few minutes later and found them still sitting in the same spot. "Jackson."

"Hey, Doc."

"I guess this is Samantha Harris." The grey hair man held out his hand. "I'm Dr. King."

"It's nice to meet you."

The doctor took a seat across from her. "I'm a specialist in substance abuse. If you want me to, I can see you throughout your treatment regimen no matter where you are. I understand you are a performer?"

"Yes, sir."

"Good. I'm assuming you travel extensively."

"Yes, sir."

"We will keep you in medication for your symptoms then and you will be able to refill them anywhere you are should you run out."

"I appreciate that." She glanced at Jackson. "This medicine will help with the tremors, nausea, headaches, and other stuff?"

"Yes, they will, but the big thing is you can't drink with them. It is important to understand the dangers in taking that path. Just like with any other medication, alcohol is a bad mixture."

"I won't. I promise."

The doctor glanced at him. "I understand you and Jackson are in a relationship?"

"Yes, sir."

"You will be monitoring her quite closely, right, son?"

"Yes. If I can prevent her from drinking at all, that's my plan."

"Good. She's going to need all the support she can get, which means everyone around her."

"Understood."

"Well then, I will leave you two to your privacy. I've called in the prescription to the local pharmacy here in Bandera for you to pick up." He stood and held out his hand.

Samantha stood as well, taking the man's hand in hers to shake. "Thank you for coming, Doctor King. I appreciate it tremendously."

"You're welcome, my dear. I hope to see you in my office in a couple of weeks if you can make it just to check up. Call me anytime though." He handed her some brochures out of his briefcase. "Here are some treatment facilities that you might look into. Even if you can't do inpatient treatment, I would suggest AA. Jacob can direct you to a local chapter although I don't know how long you'll be here before you have to travel on."

"Not long."

"I figured as much." He shot a look at Jackson. "There are AA chapters everywhere. I suggest you look up some in the areas she'll be in. She's going to need the support even if she has a sponsor here."

"Jacob agreed to be her sponsor."

"Good. He'll be a fantastic sponsor and he's been through this himself. He knows what you're going through." The man stepped around the table. "I'll take my leave. You two take care of each other. It's going to be a long hard road."

"Thank you."

As the doctor left, Jackson turned her to face him. "Are you okay?"

"Yes," she whispered. "I don't know if I can do this, Jackson."

"Sure you can, babe. I'll be there for you every step of the way."

"You keep this up, and I'm going to fall in love with you."

# Chapter Eleven

The love word scared the crap out of him. He didn't need to fall in love with anyone nor did he need someone falling in love with him. His life seemed just fine the way it was. "You shouldn't talk like that, Samantha. Your life is too much of a rollercoaster right now to be fallin' in love with anyone."

"No worries, cowboy. I'm kind of a loner."

He pushed a piece of hair back behind her ear, loving the feel of the silky strands in his fingers. "Good. I'm not sure if we would be good for each other or not anyway. I'm kind of a bossy guy."

"I don't take orders well."

"See. We totally wouldn't get along on a long-term basis." He brushed his lips against hers. "How about we go to bed?"

One of her eyebrows went up over her eye. "Bed?"

"Yeah. I mean we are pretty good together when we have sex."

"True."

"How 'bout it? I mean if you feel up to it."

"I do have a bit of a headache."

"Why don't we run into town, pick up your prescription and see how you feel later? It's still early."

"Okay."

"We could grab a bite to eat at the diner if you want, something a little more intimate than dealing with my entire family for the supper meal."

"Sounds good to me." She brushed her lipstick off his bottom lip. "I'd like to have you to myself for a bit."

"Great." He wrapped an arm around her shoulders to lead her toward the door to the outside. "My aunt will love you. I think she's a fan."

"Your aunt?"

"Yep. She owns the diner."

"Sounds great. Let me grab a couple CDs and I'll sign them for her."

"That would be fantastic. I'm sure she'll love you even more if you did."

"Let's get them from the bus. I always keep a stash on there."

"Sure."

She popped the door of the bus open a few minutes later, and took the steps up into the interior of the big motor coach. He was always struck by the clean lines of the interior of her space. It was like her, beautiful and simply designed. She wasn't really a complicated individual from what he knew of her, which granted wasn't much more than what he knew from the media. Maybe they should have that talk during supper.

Once she had several CDs in her hands, they walked back down the stairs, locked the door, and headed out to his truck to drive into town. "We'll have to hit the pharmacy first. I think they close fairly early."

"No problem."

The drive into Bandera only took about ten minutes, not long enough to really get into a conversation. He wanted to suggest going to the Dusty Boot, but he felt it wasn't a good idea with her going through withdrawals right now. The alcohol would be flowing, tempting her to throw her first chance at sobriety to the wind and drink again. He wouldn't do something so cruel to her.

He glanced at her across the truck as the bar came into view. They had to drive past it to get his aunt's diner. She licked her lips and watched closely as they drove by.

"Is that the local bar?"

"Yeah. It's where Peyton works."

"Looks busy."

"It usually is. It's really the only place to hang out in Bandera so it's hopping most of the time." He took her hand in his as he pulled into an empty spot in front of the diner. "Are you okay?"

"Yeah. It's hard, you know?"

"I can imagine."

"You are such a strong person, Jackson. I can't imagine you being weak to anything."

"I have my issues too, Samantha. I tend to be hardnosed sometimes, not giving people the benefit of the doubt in some situations." He kissed her fingers. "We can talk more inside. I'm kind of hungry."

"Me too. The food wasn't very good at the hospital."

"I can imagine." He pushed open his door and rushed around the front of the truck to open hers for her once he slammed his own shut. "My lady."

"Such a gallant gentleman. Your mother would be proud." She smiled a little crooked half grin as she palmed his cheek. "You are one of the good guys, Jackson. Any woman would be happy to call you their own."

"Someday, maybe. I'm not in a hurry."

He opened the door, holding it for her to enter as the little bell tinkled announcing their arrival. The diner was kind of slow tonight from what it looked like, but that was okay with him. Having a quiet dinner, just the two of them sounded good.

There was a long bar to the left with old fashioned round stools for the patrons to sit on who might be dining alone with several booths and tables scattered around the room, giving the diner an old fashioned feel. His Aunt Ann had run the place for as long as he could remember.

"Jackson! How the heck are you? I haven't seen you in here in a while, son." Ann hugged him with one arm as she held a coffee pot with the other. "Who's the beautiful girl?"

"Ann, this is Samantha Harris."

"Oh my!" Ann put her hand to her chest. "*The* Samantha Harris? I didn't recognize you without your hat. I'm a huge fan of yours."

"So I heard, and thank you. You are more than kind."

"Honey, you have the voice of an angel. I just love your songs. I could listen to you for hours. I have all of your CDs."

"I guess you wouldn't be interested in them signed, then huh?"

"Signed. Oh hell yeah, I would! That would be fantastic!" Ann set the coffee pot down on the counter and hugged Samantha. "I love you. You…"

Jackson thought it was kind of funny how Samantha hugged her back kind of awkwardly as she glanced over Ann's shoulder.

"What the heck are you doing here with this rascal?"

"It's a long story."

"You'll have to tell me sometime, but for now, get yourselves a booth. What would you like to drink?"

"Coke is fine for me."

"Sprite would be great if you have it."

"Certainly." Ann giggled like a total fangirl. "Samantha Harris, in my diner. Wow."

She waddled off to get their drinks as he and Samantha took a seat in one of the booths. He handed Sam a menu from behind the salt and pepper shakers. As he looked over the menu he knew by heart, a small girl with bright red hair stopped at the edge of their table.

"Are you really Samantha Harris the country singer?"

"Yes, honey, I am."

The little girl twisted a napkin in her palm. "Can I get your autograph? I love your songs."

"Sure, baby." Samantha smiled at the little girl. "Do you want it on the napkin?"

The little girl handed it over to Sam. "Uh. Yeah. Sorry. It's kind of wrinkled."

"That's okay. How about if I grab one out of our holder to sign?"

The little girl nodded so fast, her curls bounced.

"What's your name?"

"Abby."

He watched as Samantha signed it with a marker he didn't realize she had, asked the little girl to take a picture with her, and chatted with her for a few minutes. She really did love her fans from what he could tell.

"Oh." Samantha pulled out a CD from her purse. "Here is a CD for you too, since you are such a big fan."

"Wow," Abby whispered. A second later, she practically leapt into Samantha's arms as she hugged her tightly before she rushed back to her mother's side.

The woman had tears in her eyes as she mouthed, thank you over Abby's head.

"You are a sucker for fans, huh?"

"Yeah. I love meeting them and talking with them."

"You made that little girl's whole year probably."

"You think so?"

"Yeah." He grasped her hands in his. "You are a beautiful person inside and out."

She flushed red. "You're embarrassing me."

"You are easily embarrassed, but it's the truth."

"Thank you."

He reluctantly pulled his hand back to grab his menu again. Not that he needed to read it. The thing hadn't changed in twenty years, but he really needed to keep his hands busy, otherwise he might do something really stupid like grab her and kiss her right there in the diner.

Ann came to their table a minute later with their drinks. "Sorry. I didn't mean to take so long, but I didn't want to interrupt your time with Abby. She's a sweet girl for everything she's going through."

"Oh?" Samantha asked, putting her menu down.

"Yeah. She was diagnosed with Leukemia about a month ago. She's getting ready to start treatments this coming week."

"Oh my. How sad."

"Honey, you are the reason that little girl is smiling right now. Don't be sad for her. She's got a fighting spirit and great chances for remission. I bet she'll play that CD until it's plum wore out."

"Thanks, Ann, but I didn't do anything."

"Hush. Yes you did. You made that little girl's day a little brighter with your kindness. It takes a special person to be good to others. You've got it, whatever it is." Ann pulled out her pen and pad. "What are you having for supper?"

After they ordered, he sipped his Coke while he watched Samantha across the table. What Ann said was right. There was something special about this woman and he aimed to find out what it was before they were through, even if it took him the whole six weeks they would be together to figure things out.

"What?"

"Nothing, why?"

"You're staring."

"Sorry. You are a beautiful woman. I'm lucky to be sitting here with you." He set his Coke back down. "Why don't we get to know each other a little better?"

"Okay."

"What's your favorite color?"

"Green. Yours?"

"Red. Favorite flower?"

"Um, Lilies."

"Favorite song?"

"Not one of mine?" she asked, taking a sip from her drink.

"Nope."

"Stay from Little Big Town."

"Favorite movie?"

"Ghost. That one is my all-time favorites. I love Patrick Swayze." She took another drink before setting the glass back down. "Your turn. Favorite movie?"

"Remember the Titians."

"Favorite sport?"

"Hockey, but I like baseball and football too."

"Not rodeo?"

"No. I watch bull riding on television sometimes, but I think those boys are crazy." Ann came by the table with their food. Everything looked fabulous, as usual. "Thanks, Ann."

"You're welcome." She wiped her hands on the apron around her middle. "You two enjoy."

They dug into their food with gusto, enjoying the homemade food of a good cook.

"This is fabulous!"

"Ann is one of the best cooks in the area. Her diner does well through the seasons where most places would have a hard time. She's got the local crowd coming here multiple times during the week."

As Samantha shoved a forkful of potato into her mouth, she hummed her appreciation. His dick jumped at the sound, hoping she would make the same one when she sucked his cock later. It hadn't been more than a couple of days, but he wanted her with a fervor he didn't know he possessed.

"You're looking at me funny."

"I can't wait to get you back to the cabin so I can fuck you properly," he whispered. He didn't need the whole place knowing his dick was about to explode.

She slowly licked the tinges of the fork before putting them into her mouth and leisurely pulling it back out. A small piece of potato clung on her lip, making him want to lick it off with everything inside him. Her eyes twinkled with mirth as she slowly, methodically tortured him to death right there in the middle of the diner.

"So? How was supper?" Ann asked, dragging him back from his erotic thoughts.

"Fantastic as usual."

"Good. I wanted to make sure you enjoyed it."

"The food was to die for, Ann." She turned sideways in the chair to dig into her purse. "Here are the CDs I promised you. They're all signed for your collection or whatever."

"Thank you!"

"You're welcome. I hope you can come out to a show soon. I would love for you to come backstage with me and Jackson."

"I would love to. I'm not sure if you'll be around here coming up or not."

"I'd have to check my schedule. I think we are doing a show in Houston, but that might be too far for you to come."

"For you, honey, I'd go to Florida."

Samantha laughed as she leaned back in her chair. "I would love to see you."

Ann glanced back and forth between them for a minute before she grinned from ear to ear. He knew that look. His mother had a knack for matchmaking, but her sister was good at it too. "You two are cute together. I hope to see more of this."

"Hold your horses, Ann. We are getting to know each other." Though he had a sneaky suspicion he was falling in love with Samantha.

"That's the first step!" Ann grabbed their now empty plates. "Can I get you two some pie?"

"You have to have a piece of pie, Samantha. Her apple and cherry are the best."

"Okay. Apple it is."

"Two?" Ann glanced at him with a questioning look.

"Of course. I can't pass up your pie. With ice cream, please."

Samantha nodded quickly. "Oh yeah, me too. Ice cream, definitely."

"Be right back."

Samantha reached across the table and picked up his hand before bringing his fingers to her mouth.

"What are you doing?"

"Seeing if you have anything on your fingers." She licked around the end of his pinky. "Nope. Not on that one." She tried the next, and then the next.

*My cock is so hard, it hurts to breathe.* "You're killing me."

"I know. Don't you love it?"

"You'll pay for this when we get back. I'm going to torture the hell out of you."

"I hope so."

Ann returned with their pie, setting one plate down in front of each of them. "Enjoy."

Sam turned on the torture during the pie eating by licking the fork and moaning softly with each bite. She sounded like she might orgasm right there from eating pie, but the joke was on him.

With each little moan, pre-cum leaked from the end of his dick. His balls ached, and his breath came out in ragged pants.

Worst thing of all, he didn't taste one bite of his pie and ice cream.

* * * *

The ride home after they'd picked they'd eaten was torturous for Samantha. Her nipples hurt from being so tight she could key a car with them, to her pussy throbbing with each beat of her heart. Good grief, she wanted to rip his damned clothes off right there in the truck and fuck him every which way but up. She wanted to feel the fun little knob on the end of his cock, rubbing the sweet little spot inside her. She needed to have him eat her pussy until she creamed all over his face. The desire she felt for this man, scared her a little. She didn't need someone like this, this badly. *What happens when he walks away at the end of our journey?* She didn't want to think about that right now. For the immediate future, she needed to concentrate on staying sober, living her life, and finding out who the stalker was so she could move on.

When they pulled up in front of her cabin, she turned to face him on the seat. "Are you going to join me?"

"Hell yeah, I am." He frowned and then adjusted his hat on his head. "Unless you don't want me to."

"Of course I want you to, silly. I've been thinking about this all afternoon. Well, in between headaches and bouts of nausea."

"If you aren't feeling up to this, we can postpone it."

"No way. I'm hornier than a cow in heat." She laughed. "That wasn't a very sexy euphemism, was it?"

He wrinkled his nose. "Not really."

"Anyway, yes I want you to stay the night and no, I won't call you a prostitute this time."

"Good. We are okay on the money thing, right?"

"I still think you should be paid for being my bodyguard or whatever you want to call it, but no, I'm not paying you for having sex with me. That's a bonus."

"Bonus?"

"Yeah, bonus for me having your sexy-ass body all to myself for however long you are on the road with me. Score!"

He shook his head as he rolled his eyes. She knew she was being silly, but it was kind of fun to cut loose and not worry about all the business of being a singer, just for one night. Tonight, she planned to enjoy Jackson Young to the fullest of her abilities and love every minute of it.

When he came around to her side of the truck, he opened the door, and swept her up in his arms before pushing the truck door closed with his boot. A quick kiss revealed the longing in him as he walked quickly toward her cabin.

"Where's the key?"

"In my pants pocket."

"Can you reach it?"

She unlooped her hands from around his neck. The key was in her front left pocket. "Yes," she said, pulling it from the confines.

He leaned in so she could open the door. It was kind of sexy how he carried her across the threshold of the cabin before dropping her in the middle of the bed.

After he went back to shut the door, he stripped off his shirt and then went to undo his belt buckle. She licked her suddenly dry lips as he slowly peeled his jeans down to reveal his cock to her gaze. The man had it going on. His cock sprang up from the curly black hair at the base, to rest against his abdomen. The piercing fascinated her with its simplicity. The stud went through the cock itself, leaving a ball at the head of his cock and one on the underside of the head. She remembered how the thing felt against her G spot, tantalizing and rubbing the special little spot into the most amazing orgasm she'd ever felt. She knew she'd never had an orgasm from there before.

He moved close enough for her to touch without reaching out too far. "I want your mouth. I've been dreaming of those lips around my cock all day."

"Come closer." He moved next to the bed as she brought her hand to his balls, massaging the rounded nuts with her hand while the other grasped his cock at the base. "This is incredible."

"I'm glad you like it."

"And the piercing is to die for. I love it." She took him in her mouth just far enough to drag a moan from his. She flicked the little ball with her tongue, rolling it around and around until his hips rocked toward her. She knew what he wanted, but she would make him wait a little longer to get his full on blowjob. Licking and swirling, she teased her tongue up and down the shaft.

He grabbed a fistful of her hair, pulling until her scalp burned slightly. "You're killing me. Suck."

She hummed around his cock as she continued her assault on his senses. *Torture is too good for him.* She wanted him to suffer a little before she gave him what he wanted so badly. "Oh no, not yet, cowboy."

"You will so pay for this."

"I'm counting on it."

She continued to bring him to the brink of insanity, dragging out her assault, before backing him off slowly.

"God, woman. Finish it."

"All right. Since you asked so nicely."

She deep throated his cock until he bumped the back of her throat, sucking him on the way back up. Up and down she sucked, stopping every few minutes to nibble on the end of his dick.

His hips rocked into her face as he held her head in place with his hands twisted in her hair.

She loved every tug, every pull, to the point she wanted to reach down and finger her own clit to bring some relief to the pounding of her blood. She was so horny, she hurt.

A moment later, hot cum spurted out the end of his dick deep into her throat. She swallowed every drop of the sticky liquid until nothing remained.

First, his knees hit the bed beside her, before he fell face first onto the mattress.

"You okay?" she asked, running her hands down his back and right arm. She liked the tattoo scrolled over his shoulder, almost as much as she loved the piercing in his dick and the one in his nipple. "I hope you aren't done for the night?"

"Give me a minute."

"Of course." She sat up on the side of the bed before stripping off her clothes and boots. Once she had everything off, she climbed back onto the mattress, spread her legs, and began to slowly finger her clit.

He turned toward her and opened his eyes. "Damn woman."

"What?"

"That is about the sexiest thing I've ever seen."

She brought her fingers to her mouth, wet the surface and then returned to her clit. "You've never seen a woman masturbate?"

"A time or two. I love to watch you anyway I can though."

"I hope you plan on eating me, because I *really* like when you do that."

He rolled onto his side and propped himself up on his elbow. She glanced down at his cock, amazed it had begun to get hard again.

"You do have some stamina for an old guy."

"Old?"

"You're what? Like thirty-five, right?"

"Yeah, so?"

"Women are in there prime during their thirties and forties. Men are usually on the downhill slide at your age."

"I'll show you downhill slide."

He jumped toward her so fast, she squealed, laughing hilariously as she tried to get away. He quickly tackled her on to the bed with his body weight, pinning her arms near her sides.

His lips did a slow crawl from her mouth to her ear. "I've got more than you can handle, babe."

"I'm hoping so. I want you to fuck me so hard, we break the bed."

"Break the bed, huh?"

"I'll buy a new one if you do."

"Sounds like a plan to me."

He scooted down her body, dragging his lips along her chest until he reached her right nipple. The jutting tip stood taut, waiting for his mouth to close over it. He ran his teeth over the end, dragging a moan from her mouth that sounded like something dragged from deep inside her chest.

"Oh God."

"Master will do."

"Yeah, no."

"Party pooper." He raked his teeth over the other nipple. "I can do this all night."

"I hope so. Good God, I hope so."

He continued to trail his mouth down her abdomen until he reached the juncture of her thighs. The first touch of his tongue on her clit, drove her hips straight up until he pressed them back to the bed with his hands on her hip bones. "Easy, darlin."

She loved when he called her that.

*The man has a wicked tongue totally meant to pleasure a woman, not just any woman, me specifically.*

Pleasure darted through her as he worked her clit, flicking it, sucking it, and moving it back and forth. He definitely knew his way around a woman's body.

His fingers rolled her right nipple, shooting desire straight to her pussy. Her heart raced, beating wildly inside her chest. Her nipples burned, pulling into tight little nubs. The muscles of her abdomen quivered as the soft touch of his fingers tickled the skin.

Her body went on high alert as he pushed two fingers into her pussy, slowly pumping them in and out. He licked her clit, rolling the tiny nub with his tongue.

"Ever had a man in your ass?"

"Mmm. Yes." Her breathing seesawed in a rapid rhythm as she whispered the words. "One of my favorite positions."

He slipped a third finger into her back hole.

"Good. I love the position too."

Her whole body hurt from the need to come. "Please, Jackson. Make me come."

"I plan to. In a minute or twenty."

"I can't stand it!" The slow lick of his tongue on her clit held her on the edge of a climax.

"It'll be that much more powerful when you do."

"You're such a tease."

"Yep." He moved back. "Roll over."

She flipped around so her ass was in the air. Good Lord, she needed this more than anything to take the edge off. Her life seemed to have done a nosedive in the last couple of days. Relief in the way of a mind-blowing orgasm would help tremendously. "Do it."

"Give me a second. I need a condom and some lube."

"Lube is in the drawer. Hurry. I'm dying here."

Seconds later, she felt the head of his cock bump against the puckered hole of her ass as cold liquid dribbled down her crack. She knew the burn would be painful, but she didn't care. She needed this, needed the pain to reset her brain from the rapid firing thoughts bouncing around in there.

The first slide of his penetration made her suck in her breath.

"Relax."

"I'm trying."

With one palm on each butt cheek, he worked her ass farther apart as he moved past the ring of muscles.

"Oh yeah."

"I'm almost in."

"Give me all of it. I need this. I need you."

He pushed steadily until he was all the way in and she felt the brush of his hair against her butt.

"Yes."

"I feel so full. You're a big guy."

"Feels fantastic."

"Move, please." The deliberate, slow in and out rhythm of his thrusts would drive her to climax in seconds if he kept it up much longer. "Faster."

"I don't want to hurt you. You're very tight."

"Please."

He increased his pace until he was slamming against her ass in a body jarring motion, however, the minute he reached around and fingered her clit, she exploded into shards of herself as her world centered on what he was doing to her body. Her mind floated out and around them, bringing her into a peaceful, drifting feeling.

Several minutes later, he shouted his own release as he pushed against her ass in a jagged tempo. They both went down on the bed as he collapsed on her back.

# Chapter Twelve

The next several days were spent making love, finding out more about Jackson and his family, and general relaxation. She knew they would be back to the crazy schedule of the road soon. She wasn't looking forward to it anymore. Yeah, it would be great to have Jackson with her, but the daily grind of moving from one place to the other every couple of days just didn't appeal anymore. Maybe it was time to hang up her microphone. Her manager, agent, and record label would have a fit. She needed to do what she needed to do for her sanity though.

She licked her lips. The days had went by fairly quick even without the alcohol to numb her brain. She actually felt pretty good on the medication when she needed it, which wasn't really all that often. Occasionally, she would have an anxiety attack, freak out a little, and need her pill, but Jackson knew how to bring her down from those episodes.

This morning she sat on her bus plucking out a few new lyrics and chords to a song she was writing. She really liked where this one seemed to be headed. It fit her life at the moment, even though it was a love song.

Love song.

She tapped the pencil to her lips. What the hell to do about Jackson Young. He had become more important to her life as the days went by. What would happen when they spent several weeks in close contact on her bus? Lots of love making, she hoped, but was afraid that would be detrimental to her heart.

If she admitted it to herself, she was already half in love with the cowboy. This wouldn't do. She didn't want to drag someone into this crazy life with her. She knew she could trust him though, and she knew he wasn't after her money or fame. He had his own life. Did it include her, she wondered as she went back to doodling on the paper. When she looked down, she realized she'd written Jackson's name along with her own, several times.

She blew out a breath as she put the pencil down. Getting into a relationship with him wasn't really a good idea, but she couldn't seem to help herself. Relationship, real or fake, it didn't matter, they were in it now whether she wanted to believe it or not.

A knock sounded on the door.

"Come in."

The door opened and Jacob peeked inside the bus. "How are you doing?"

"I'm good. Come on up."

Jacob climbed the stairs in quick secession. "Wow. Nice."

"Thanks."

"Is this what you travel in all the time?"

"Yeah. I need my comforts, I guess. It has to be home for several weeks at a time." She motioned to the couch across from her. "Have a seat and tell me what brings you to my humble abode."

He took a seat on the white leather couch, pulling at the thighs of his jeans. She could definitely tell Jacob and Jackson were brothers. They both had the dark hair, sexy face, and penetrating stare, not that they both were amazing to look at. Jackson wore facial hair where most of his brothers didn't. Plus, he had that awesome tribal tattoo from his shoulder to his wrist swirling around his arm.

"I wanted to check on you. I know it's been a few days since you had your last drink. It's usually the roughest the first few days, but it can also last for several weeks."

"I'm doing okay. I've had a few anxiety episodes. The medication helps." She set the guitar next to her on the floor. "I think the big test will be when we get on the road."

"You are still taking Jackson, right?"

"Yes, if he wants to. I won't force him, of course."

Jacob laughed. "I don't think you could force him to do anything he didn't want to do. He's about the most stubborn of all of us, although I'm not sure my mother would agree."

She laughed a little as she glanced down at her hands. "I do appreciate you asking about me. You don't have to keep such a close eye on me though. I think I've got this handled."

One eyebrow shot up over his eye. "You think so?"

"Yep. I've been clean and sober for a week. I've got this." She nodded, confident she could handle her life without booze or pills.

He frowned. "There will be a time you'll be tested on that theory. Just remember, I'm here, Peyton is here, and Jackson too. We are all here to help you get past this." He dangled his hands between his knees. "Have you contacted an AA group or went to one of their meetings?"

"No. I don't need those people. Besides, I have to be careful this doesn't get out into the media. It could kill my career if they knew I had an alcohol problem."

"Have, Samantha. You have an alcohol problem. You have to think of this as an ongoing issue. I haven't had a drink since Paige rescued me at the bar. I still have an alcohol problem. It isn't something that goes away with time. It will always be a problem in your life and something you have to battle constantly. Are there days I want a drink? Yep, and it's something I fight daily."

"Really?"

"Yes. Please don't think this is an issue you can just stop without realizing it will always be with you. You'll fail if you do. That's the last thing I want for you."

She bit the left side of the inside of her mouth as she looked at the paper she'd been writing on. "You've given me a lot to think about. I hope I can make all of you proud of me, but I didn't think of this in that way. I thought once I quit, I wouldn't have the problem anymore. That it was done, but it sounds like that's not the case."

"You have to understand. It is a difficult journey to go through and it definitely is something you will require help with. You will feel weak. You will want a drink. You will possibly fail, but you have to get back up and try again."

"I'm ready, Jacob. I really am. I need to get over this fear of performing to realize I am talented, I am a good person, and I can entertain people. I have to get past people being jealous of my success. They want me to fail, but I won't. I'm better than that."

"Yes, you are. You're a great performer. Your fans love you." He slowly climbed to his feet. "I will leave to you write. I know you are working on some new material."

"I am." She turned the paper over, not wanting him to see her doodles on the sheet. "It's kind of private though."

He smiled. She had a feeling he'd already seen her drawings. "I won't ask you how your relationship with Jackson is going. I know he can be kind of an ass."

"He's great, actually. Things are progressing, and I'm sure we'll have a great time on the road. I think he'll be right in his element guarding me. He seems to be the type to like to take charge."

"That he is, definitely." He walked toward the stairs. "If you need me, call. You have my number."

"Yes, I do. Thank you."

He tipped his hat and headed out of the bus, leaving her wondering. Did she really think this whole thing would blow over? Did she believe she had a drinking problem or not? If not, then she was going about this all wrong. She shrugged and turned over the paper she'd been writing the song on, going over it one more time. It was finished other than the intro chords to lead up to the words.

After she finished this, she needed to get the bus ready. They were leaving to head to California first thing in the morning. Mark would be flying back into San Antonio today and Jackson was on his way to pick him up at the airport. The band's bus had been parked at a storage lot in San Antonio and she'd already sent the guys' driver to get it ready to leave in the morning. He could sleep on the bus until he picked the guys up at the airport. They were all to meet at a central rendezvous point outside of town to head out. They would hit the road together. The first show had been scheduled in San Francisco, which was a good twenty-five hours on a good day, with buses it would take longer. The big trucks would make their way there from Nashville, where she'd sent them to go through the equipment and make sure everything was set for this tour. They would be doing a couple of shows a week for the next six weeks with only travel time between each venue. Luckily, they had booked them so it wouldn't be too hard to get from one to the other on a short time schedule.

A knock on the door brought her attention back to the task at hand. "Come in."

Jackson and Mark climbed the stairs.

"Hey, darlin'."

Her toes curled. "Hey, how was the trip? Not too much traffic, I hope."

"No, not much. Mark was already waiting when I got to the baggage claim, so it was a quick pick up and back on the road."

"Mark, I've already booked you a room in the main lodge for tonight so we'll be ready to roll out in the morning."

"Thanks."

"How was your break?"

"Good. I did a little fishin', some huntin', and a lot of relaxing. I'm ready to punch out this tour. You?"

"I'm doing better. I've quit drinking."

Mark looked surprised. "Really? I didn't think you were drinking that much."

"Well, I was. I landed in the hospital for a couple of days for it. Jackson here, helped me turn things around."

Mark glanced at Jackson with a bit of a frown on his face. "He did, huh?"

"Yep. With the help of him and his family, I've been sober for over a week. No more drinking. In fact, if you see me with anything alcoholic, stop me, please."

"Sure." His glance moved between her and Jackson several time before shooting back to her. "Does that mean the band and I have to stay clean too?"

"No, but I would appreciate it if you didn't drink around me. This is going to be hard enough."

"Sure, doll."

"What are you working on?" Jackson asked, taking the seat beside her.

"Nothing much. A new song," she said, turning the paper over quickly.

"Can I see it?"

"No."

"Why not? I'm one of your biggest fans, remember?"

"I know, but I don't like people seeing what I've got going until I'm done and it's been polished."

"Polished as in adding all the strings, horns, and other various instruments so it's ready to be recorded?"

"Something like that, yeah." She stuffed the paper at the bottom of her guitar case, put the guitar inside, and closed the lid. "You'll hear it when it's done."

"Have you been rehearsing?"

"Yeah, some. I have all the songs down I want to do at the show this weekend, but I'll go over them again while we are on the road." She took a sip of the Coke sitting on the table. "Can I get you guys something to drink?"

"I'm good," Mark replied. "I'm going to do a quick walk around on the bus and make sure everything looks okay. We don't want to break down anywhere."

"Good idea," Jackson said as Mark took the steps down to the exterior or the bus.

"Was he this talkative on the road back from the airport?"

"Yeah, pretty much. I don't think he said two words to me."

She pressed her lips together. "He's never been this quiet before. He usually runs off at the mouth a lot while we are driving, telling me stories, making me laugh, and keeping me company."

"You sound pretty close."

"Well, most of the time it's just the two of us on the bus since the guys in the band have their own." She shrugged as she looked out the front window. "I guess. He's like a brother to me."

"Good to know."

"No worries, Jackson. You are my guy."

"At least for now."

"For now."

The bell clanged for supper. "You ready to eat?"

"Yeah. I've been working for a while. I'm kind of hungry."

He took her hand and brought it to his lips for a kiss to the back. "Let's go get some food then. We'll grab Mark on the way out."

After dinner, she sat next to Jackson on the couch in the front room of the lodge, sipping a cup of coffee, and watching the flames dance in the fireplace. She probably shouldn't have been drinking it because the caffeine would keep her awake when it was bedtime, but she wanted to finish the song she'd been working earlier. The words drifted back to her mind, bringing a smile to her lips.

"What's the smile for?"

"I'm thinking about the song I was working on earlier."

"That good?"

"I think so. I really believe it will be a hit on my next CD."

"When do you start recording it?"

"After this next six weeks is up. I have some time booked in the studio to work on it."

"How long does it take to record a CD?"

"About a year or year and a half. It depends on how fast I find the songs I want to record, how easy they are to get, and how well the recording goes." She took another drink of her coffee, before putting it on the coffee table. *This being sober thing is going pretty well. I haven't even really wanted a drink in a day or two. I think I've got this licked.*

Jackson's fingers did a slow crawl across the back of her neck, sending shivers down her arms. Had it really only been since last night since they'd had sex? She was becoming addicted to his brand of loving. She really liked the wicked things his tongue did to her clit.

"What am I going to need to do for you while we are on the road?"

"Make sure no one gets near me that's not supposed to."

"Kind of like what I did at the charity concert?"

"Yeah, although you'll have full access to my bus, the band's bus, and the rigs with the equipment, but the main thing is guarding me."

"That I can do." He nuzzled her neck near her ear.

"Are you ready for bed?"

"Always with you."

"Shall we head here then?"

"Um, I really need to get this song done."

"Are you turning me down for sex?"

She cringed as she said, "Yes, and no. Later?"

He laughed as he kissed her ear. "Later is fine. I know you want to work on the song you're writing."

"Thank you. You are a very special guy."

"No thanks needed. I can work on some stuff in my room. I need to pack anyway so we can leave first thing in the morning."

"I need to do that too. I've got stuff strung all over the cabin."

"Looks like a typical woman's room to me every time I see it."

She drank the last dregs of her coffee before she stood. Jackson climbed to his feet beside her. They dropped their coffee cups in the dirty dish bin on their way to the door. As they went their separate ways in the dark, she wondered how on earth she'd managed to find such a great guy.

Several hours later, she tapped her booted foot as she strummed the guitar, humming the melody to herself as she closed her eyes, letting the music flow through her. She had it. The final version of the song was completed. It was perfect and she knew her manager, her agent, her records producer, and most of all Jackson would love it. Excitement skittered through her. She wanted to play it for him now, but then again, she didn't. She wanted to let the musicians do their thing before she let him hear it, kind of as a surprise.

She glanced down at the paper at the last lyric.

*I love you.*

Did she? Did she really fall in love with Jackson Young in ten days? Wasn't that kind of strange? She wasn't sure and she really wished she had someone she could call and talk to about it, but it was one in the morning now and everyone she knew had already long gone to bed. She quickly glanced out the front window of the bus, noticing Jackson's light still burned.

Depression set in as she saw the light go out moments later. She didn't want to disturb him now that he'd gone onto bed, but she really needed him tonight. Nerves had begun to shake her when she thought about performing in a few days' time. How would she be able to get on that stage, rock the house, and play it well for the fans without having a little liquid courage ahead of time?

She chewed her lip as she thought about having a drink. She really needed one right now to calm things down, but she wouldn't. *Go onto bed and sleep it off.* That's what she'd do. She was stronger than they thought she was. Handling this alcohol thing wasn't easy, but she could do it, she knew she could.

After playing through the song one more time, she allowed a tear to slip down her cheek. Yep, she'd gone and fallen in love with the cowboy and now she had to figure out how to turn their relationship into something real.

The question tonight was whether to slip into his room, ravish his naked body, and leave him with a smile on his lips until morning or let him sleep.

Her pussy creamed at the thought of silently stroking his cock to hardness, taking him into her mouth as she tongued the wicked little piercing, and then riding his hips until he came so hard, he saw stars. Sounded like a plan to her.

*I hope he left his door unlocked.*

She laughed as she set the guitar aside before climbing to her feet. By the time she'd made it outside to the ground, she was grinning like a Cheshire cat who'd swallowed a canary. The winter evening had turned colder. She rubbed her arms to ward off the chill.

With her key, she locked the bus, before heading in the direction of his cabin. She silently tiptoed onto the wooden porch, careful not to make a sound. The doorknob easily turned under her hand as she sent up a thankful prayer, glad he'd left it unlocked.

Moonlight streamed through the window over his head, illuminating his body on the bed. He had one arm draped over his eyes, the sheet pulled down to expose his naked chest, and the rest of it bunch around his hips. She would easily be able to slowly peel it off him without waking him.

She silently closed the door, being careful not to wake him. After she quickly toed off her boots, she moved on stocking feet to the side of the bed.

His leg moved and she held her breath. A soft snore reached her ears. She smiled thinking about what would go through his mind when he awoke to her mouth on his cock.

She slipped off her clothes as quietly as possible, and then moved toward the bed. The sheet looked bunched around his hips, but loose enough she should be able to free his cock to her touch. Giving it a little tug, she managed to free his hips from the sheet, thankful he slept nude.

His cock was semi-hard, lying against his stomach. The ball on the end near the slit glistened in the moonlight. Her fingers itched to touch him all over. She wanted to run her hands from his pierced nipple to his cock, smoothing her palms over his contours and valleys. Tonight, she would do that even if it meant tying his hands to the headboard. Touching him gave her such pleasure and now that she'd given into her feelings by admitting to herself she was in love with him, it took on a whole new meaning.

She smoothed her fingertip over the end of his cock. He didn't stir although his dick twitched. She smiled.

Bent over at the waist, she licked around the metal ball before flicking her tongue over the head of his cock. He moaned softly.

Taking his balls in her palm, she worked them with her fingers as she took the head of his cock in her mouth and sucked.

"You are a little witch coming in here like this after leaving me hanging until early morning."

"You love it," she whispered against his now fully erect dick. "I wanted to take advantage of you in your sleep."

"You did."

She deep throated his cock, allowing the ball to bump the back of her throat. A deep hum vibrated the skin on his cock as she went up and down on the hard shaft. Sucking his cock really did it for her in the most primal way. It was her way of giving him pleasure beyond the norm before she received her own pleasure from him. She wanted to take care of him, love him, and make him see her as something besides a woman needing him to take care of her.

"I wanted to give you something for everything you're doing for me. I'm going to suck you until you almost come, then I'm going to ride you until you explode inside me."

"Sounds like a plan." He wound his hands in her loose hair, guiding her mouth as she continued to suck and play with his cock.

His soft moans echoed in the quiet room. His little words of encouragement and endearments made her heart sing. Maybe he did feel something for her after all even if it wasn't love, yet.

"Okay, enough. I can't take it. I need to be inside you."

"Condom?"

"In the drawer."

She grabbed one out of the drawer next to the bed, grabbed his cock, and then rolled the slippery latex down over his impressive erection.

The moment she had him sheathed, she straddled his hip, and positioned his cock before slowly sliding his length inside her. The feeling was incredible. He fit so perfectly, she couldn't help but wonder if they were made for each other. Surely so. Everything about him did it for her, his kindness, his caring, the way he made love, the way he took care of his family, the way he did for others, and mostly the way he took care of her. He'd done so much for her since they had met, it was no wonder she'd fallen in love with him.

"Ride me, darlin'."

As she began to move her hips, the glide of his cock felt absolutely wonderful. The little ball hit something inside her, sending her senses into overdrive, her pussy into spasms on the verge of climax, and her nipples to throbbing with every beat of her heart. She gasped as he palmed both her breasts in his hands, massaging the globes as she threw back her head. Her nipples burned for his touch. "Roll them. Pluck them. I need the pain."

"My pleasure. I love your boobs."

She moaned as she leaned back to brace her hands on his thighs while she continued to ride his cock like a bucking-bronc rider in the rodeo.

"You feel fantastic. Squeeze me," he said, rolling her nipples between his thumb and first finger.

She did a few Kegel maneuvers.

"Oh yeah, that's perfect. Do it again."

Desire skittered down her back. Need ripped through her groin, making her clit throb more as she continued to ride him. His left hand skimmed down her front to settle between her legs.

The next thing she felt was his thumb rubbing her clit in rhythm to her movements. It was an amazing feeling. All the emotions she'd kept bottle up burst forth. A gut wrenching sob bubbled from her lips as she shifted forward to lean over his chest.

"Are you okay? I didn't hurt you, did I?"

"No."

"What's wrong, baby?"

"Nothing. I just…"

"Tell me."

She hesitated for several minutes. Could she tell him the truth and risk him leaving? Should she lie about what was in her heart, hoping he would chose to love her sometime in the future? Unable to hold it in any longer, she blurted, "I love you, Jackson. I know it's not the time or place for this, but I can't hold it in anymore. I need you in my life. I want you to be with me always. It's okay if you don't feel the same way. In time maybe—"

"Darlin', you've come to mean more to me than life itself over the days we've spent together. I never, ever thought I would find someone I could spend the rest of my life with or even wanted to spend more than a month with, but you're it. I've realized that I need you. You are everything to me and something I never thought I'd say to any women is I love you too."

She sighed heavily as her heart lifted. He loved her too. Wow. This was more than she ever imagined when she came to San Antonio for the benefit concert. Never in her life did she think she'd find the man of her dreams here.

"Better?"

She sniffed as she wiped her face. "Yeah."

"Good. I'm dyin' here."

"Sorry. I kind of lost it there for a minute."

"I'm sure you didn't get yours either so if you don't mind, ride me until we both get to come."

"Yes, sir." She pushed herself up on his chest, scooting her knees a little closer to his hips, and lifted herself up until his cock barely stayed inside her. "How do you want it?"

"Any way you wanna give it me."

She squeezed her muscles as she slowly took him insider her body. God, she loved his cock almost as much as she loved him. Wouldn't it be great to have him all the time? What a life they'd have. They can travel to her shows together, buy a big place in Nashville or somewhere and have a fantastic life together.

He wouldn't mind moving from Thunder Ridge. She just knew it. It would be perfect.

# Chapter Thirteen

The next morning found them on the bus with Mark at the wheel, Jackson relaxing on the white leather sofa, and Samantha picking away at her guitar.

They had only been on the road a few hours and he was bored beyond bored as he watched her pick out chords before jotting something down on the paper.

Yeah, he loved her. He would have to get used to this kind of thing, he guessed. Life with her wouldn't be boring, that's for sure. Well, maybe except for this traveling shit. He would have to take up some kind of hobby, otherwise he'd go crazy. Maybe they could hook up a horse trailer to the back of her bus and take his horse along so he'd have something to do.

An instrument?

He could always take up playing something, although he was kind of old to be learning to play. He'd had a guitar once years ago. It didn't amount to much, but if he remember right, he'd been pretty good at Mary Had a Little Lamb.

"What are you smiling about?" she asked as she glanced up.

"Nothing."

"There has to be something behind your little grin."

"I was thinking about taking up the guitar again. I had one when I was a kid, but I didn't do much with it. I played a mean Mary Had a Little Lamb."

She laughed. "It's not hard. I didn't start playing until I got my record deal."

"Yeah, but you are musically inclined. I'm not."

"We could write songs together."

"I could do lyrics while you do the melody. I'm pretty good at poetry."

"Really? That's fabulous!"

"Why don't you give me what you already have down, and I can see what I can come up with."

For the next couple of hours, they bounced ideas on lyrics off each other as the miles rolled by. It was actually a lot of fun for him. It definitely wasn't something he thought he would be doing. You know, writing songs wasn't really up his alley, but apparently it was.

"Wow. That's awesome. We totally have the song lyrics down in a couple of hours."

"I had a blast working the words out with you."

"You are pretty good at lyrics, you know? You could make a living at writing them for songs while others create the music."

"Nah. It's okay to do it for you, but I don't think it's for me on a regular basis for someone else."

"It's okay. I'll keep you to myself."

During their little writing session, he'd moved over to sit next to Samantha so they could share the paper she'd been writing music on as she hummed a melody. Now, he glanced at Mark who met his gaze in the rearview mirror over his head. Mark had a deep frown on his face and Jackson wondered why. The other man bugged him, if he was honest with himself. Nothing specific triggered the feelings that he could think of, but Mark just rubbed him wrong.

"Are you friends with any artist who plays country music?"

"A few, but a lot of them feel I didn't pay my dues before making it big, so they shun me in public."

"Well, that sucks. Who are you friends with?"

"Jason Aldean, Kellie Pickler, and a few others. Most of the big names don't want to have anything to do with me."

"Their loss."

She put her hand on his cheek. "You are too sweet. No wonder, I love you."

"I love you too." He leaned in a kissed her on the lips, before glancing back at the mirror again. Mark looked up and frowned again. *What the hell is his problem?*

"Hey, wanna go in the back and mess around?"

"Sure. The rocking of the bus should make for an interesting thrusting motion."

She set her guitar aside before grabbing his hand as she jumped to her feet. "Let's go."

For the next few hours they lost themselves in each other as they cuddled, kissed, made love, and enjoyed cocooning themselves in their own private little bedroom in the back of the bus. The world faded away as Jackson held her against his side, stroking her soft skin as she slept soundly next to him.

He knew she didn't sleep well even with the anxiety meds she had. With her brain always working, he figured it was difficult for her to rest. The alcohol had helped her so much since her career took off, the time it would take for her to get past the cravings would be a long haul. Now, he would be here for her for the rest of his life.

A smile crept across his lips. He never thought he would fall in love with anyone, much less Samantha Harris. She was perfect for him though. They had a lot in common, they loved helping people, they enjoyed the same things, and he couldn't picture his life without her. Was marriage on the horizon? He figure eventually, yeah, he would ask her to marry him, but he wanted her to get past all this shit with her alcohol problem and her nervousness of getting up in front of people to sing without the booze on board. She had a long road to go yet.

She stirred in her sleep as she rolled to her other side. He spooned in behind her as he felt the bus slow. They must be stopping for something. She opened her eyes as she rolled back toward him. "We're stopping."

"Yeah. I'll check with Mark to see what's up. Someone probably has to take a piss or something."

She pushed her hair out of her face. "It's almost dinner time anyway. We should get food. I didn't get a chance to grocery shop and stock the bus."

He was already up putting his pants on. "I'll radio the others and see what they want to do. You don't have to get up yet."

Before the words were out of his mouth, she sat up in the bed with the sheet clutched to her breasts. "I'm awake now."

"Okay." He opened the door to the bedroom as the bus rolled to a stop. With it firmly shut behind him, he walked toward the front as Mark hopped out of the driver's seat. "Where are we?"

"At a rest stop, slugger." He glanced at Jackson's lack of shirt and bare feet. "The driver of one of the rigs needed to stop."

Jackson crossed his arms over his chest. "Samantha wants to get supper. Talk to the guys and we can stop in the next town for something to eat."

"No problem." Mark didn't move.

"Is there something you want to say?"

"What's going on with you and Samantha?"

"What's it look like? We are a couple, have been since the charity benefit concert a few weeks ago."

Mark raised an eyebrow. "Let me get something off my chest. I don't like you. I think you are after her money, and you are nothing but a low-down, no good cowboy looking for a quick bit of fun. I'm keeping my eye on you, cowboy. Don't hurt her."

"Or what?"

"You'll answer to me. I've been with her for a long time. She's special to me, if you know what I mean."

"I think so."

"Then do what I tell you and no one will get hurt."

"Are you threatening me?"

"It's a promise, cowboy, not a threat." Mark spun on his heels and went down the stairs.

The bus door slammed behind him a minute later.

"What was that all about?" Samantha asked, coming out of the back in a robe.

"Nothing."

"It didn't sound like nothing."

"Do you always walk around in a bathrobe?"

"No, but I heard the door slam so I thought I should check it out."

"Do you have anything on under there?"

"Yeah, bra and panties. Is there a problem?"

"I don't think you should be walking around in a bathrobe in front of Mark."

"Mark is like a brother to me. I told you before. Besides, he's not even in here."

"He was."

"He's not now. I knew he left before I came out. Get off your high horse, Jackson. It's fine."

"It's not fine."

"What's really bugging you?"

"Nothing."

She put her hand on his face. "Nothing? It doesn't sound like it. I love you. It doesn't matter what anyone else sees, hears, or does. I'm yours."

"We still have a stalker to worry about, Samantha. It could be anyone, including Mark."

"That's crazy. Mark wouldn't think of me as anything more than an annoying sister."

"We need to start watching everyone, checking on everyone, that means all your band, your roadies, drivers, anyone else who is close to you. It could even be a fan, which would make it that much harder to track."

"Wow. I hadn't even though of those people."

"Have you done background checks on everybody?" He slipped his hands around her waist to take her into his embrace.

"No. Most came as recommended from someone else on the crew. It can't be one of my crew guys. They're all friends."

"It could be anyone."

She kissed his lips briefly and then stepped back. "I'm going to get dressed."

"I already told Mark you wanted to get some food. One of the rig drivers needed to stop so they are having a cigarette or something out there behind the buses. I'll put a shirt and my boots on so I can make sure they all know we are stopping for food."

"Good idea." She smiled. "Don't worry. We'll catch whoever it is."

"I hope so. It worries me that you are so vulnerable."

"I'm not with you around."

"I'm only one man."

"But you are my man. I love you."
"I love you too."

\* \* \* \*

The whole situation got on his nerves. He wanted to protect her and he was doing the best he could, but they still didn't know who the stalker might be. His gut told him it was someone on her team, but he hadn't been able to nail down the culprit yet.

His gaze swept the back around where they set up camp for the show in San Francisco. They had arrived earlier in the day, parked all the vehicles and got security ready to roll. Samantha had a sound check to do in the next thirty minutes while he stood guard outside her bus to make sure no one went in there without his permission.

It had been a steady stream of visitors since they arrived. Everyone from the coordinator of the show, to promotions, to the bands members needing her time, which shoved him to the outside looking in. He didn't like it, but it was something he would have to get used to. Right now the band was on the bus going through the playlist from what he could gather as he paced from the back to the front.

Darryl met him at the door after his next pass.

"Can you tell Sam and the guys we need them to sound check in a few minutes?"

"Sure." Jackson glanced at the twenty-something guy. "How long have you been one of Sam's roadies?"

"For a while now. She's so talented. I just love to listen to her sing." The kid gave him a once over. "Hey, aren't you the guy who did security for her at the charity concert a few weeks ago?"

"Yeah. I'm her permanent personal bodyguard now."

The kid frowned. "I didn't think she needed a personal bodyguard. Is there a problem?"

"Maybe. It seems there is someone who wants to get a little too close to her. My job is to keep them at bay."

"Hmm." Darryl shrugged. "She's a nice person. I'm sure whoever it is doesn't want to hurt her or anything. He might just want to have a little one-on-one with her, if you know what I mean. Nothing wrong with that, right?"

Jackson took a little closer notice of the kid. He couldn't be more than five-foot-five, skinny as a rail, with nerdy type glasses perched on his nose. "What exactly do you do for Sam?"

"I keep everything straight during set up and make sure she's on stage on time. She's late all the time if I don't stay on top of her."

"Oh?"

"Yeah. It's my job to remind her when it's time to go on and make sure she gets out there ready to perform. I'm an important part of her life, you know?"

"I can see that." Jackson frowned. He didn't like the way this kid made it sound like he was indispensable to Samantha. "I'll tell her and make sure she's out there in a few minutes."

"Thanks, man." The kid waved as he walked away. "Nice talking to you."

"You too."

Jackson knocked on the bus door, listening for her soft command to come in. When he took the stairs up, he was surprised to see the large group of people in the small space. He didn't think they could fit that many in there, but apparently, they did. "You need to do your sound check in a few."

"Thanks, baby." She smiled as she set her guitar down. "We'll be right out. Right guys?"

A chorus of affirmatives followed her statement as the men began to rise and shuffle toward the door.

Jackson stepped back as the group of men filed out, leaving Samantha standing alone in the middle of the bus. "Are you ready for this?"

"Yeah. The sound checks are okay. I don't know about the actual concert though."

He wrapped his arms around her, tucking her head under his chin. "You'll do great, darlin'. You are very talented."

"Thanks."

"You're welcome." He stepped back. "Now go get your sound check done so you can relax for a few hours before the concert begins. I have some security stuff to check on."

"Sure, baby, and thank you for having my back."

"I'll always have your back, your front, and both sides."

"I love you."

"I love you too."

She walked down the stairs and out the front of the bus as he watched her head toward the stage. He knew she would be fine, but she didn't, and he really hoped he could get her through this first concert.

Jackson took a seat at the laptop on the table and started typing in some names. He wanted to know as much about Mark Rogers and Darryl Minsky as he could find.

After about an hour of doing some research on the two men, he hadn't come up with much. Neither had a

criminal background and both had references that
checked out before they had come to work for
Samantha. There wasn't anything he could pin his
feelings on, but he knew in his gut one of the two men
was involved in this stalker thing, but which one?

Samantha returned to the bus several minutes later.
"That was fantastic! The sound is awesome in this
place. Acoustics are fabulous."

"Great, honey."

She twirled in a circle with her arms out. "You
don't understand, Jackson. I haven't played anywhere
this nice before. There will be at least ten-thousand
people in attendance at this concert and they are here to
see me!"

"I know."

She flopped down on the couch with her arms
resting on the back, letting out a huge sigh. "I should
call my parents."

"Why?"

"I always talk to them before a show, you know,
kind of a pep talk sort of thing."

"Then by all means, call them. I need to do security
rounds so I'll be back, but if I'm not back before you go
on, I love you. You'll do great."

"I love you too, Jackson. You are everything to
me."

He kissed her long and hot. Man, he really did love
this woman. He couldn't wait to see how tonight's
show went. He had a feeling she was going to knock
'em dead.

Time came for the concert to start and he was stuck
watching the back of the stage when it was Samantha's
turn to go on. The lights went low. The fog machine

started blowing smoke from the back of the stage toward the front. The crowd went wild with cheers.

He saw her walk half way up the stairs toward the back and then stop. He could see her waiver but knew she had to do this herself as much as he wanted to go to her side, hold her tight and encourage her. He'd done all he could do.

She finally took the last two stairs up to the top of the platform. She smiled back in his direction before she walked out onto the stage to the roar of the crowd.

"How is everyone tonight?"

The crowd went wild.

"Sounds like ya'll are ready to par-tay?" She turned toward the band. "Let's rock the house!"

He watched her perform from the rear of the stage, making sure no one on the floor climbed up. Security had her back with several guys stationed on the floor, two big bouncers off the side of the stage, and him. If the need arose, he would grab her and protect her with his life.

She was on the last few songs of her set when all hell broke loose.

Her boot caught on an exposed plank sending her careening off the front of the stage down into the pit area. Jackson flew past everyone, dove feet first off the platform and was near her side in a heartbeat. "Honey, are you hurt?"

She was out cold. He looked her over from head to toe, noting the funny angle of her right ankle. *Shit, it's probably broken.* "Call an ambulance. Now!" He glanced at security. "Get these people out of here. Concert is over."

One of the band got on the mic and made an announcement that the concert was over and everyone needed to file out. He told them Samantha would be okay, but they were calling an ambulance to make sure.

Jackson touched her neck to check her pulse, and leaned in to feel her breath on his face. The distinctive scent of whiskey met his nose. *Fucking son of a bitch. She's been drinking.*

"Samantha?"

She moaned softly as she moved her head from side to side, but didn't wake up fully.

*She probably has a concussion on top of a broken ankle.*

The band and security made a wide circle around her.

Someone asked, "Is she okay?"

"I'm not sure. I'm not a paramedic, but I think her ankle is broken, plus she's not waking up right away so she might have a concussion."

Her eyes fluttered open. "What's going on?" Her hand went to the back of her head and came away with blood. "Fuck."

"Lay still, darlin'. You fell off the stage. We've got paramedics on the way." As the words left his mouth, he heard sirens in the distance. "Sounds like they are close."

"What happened?"

"You must have hooked your boot on something. You tumbled off the stage."

"My ankle hurts."

"I think it's broken, baby. Don't move."

Tears smeared her mascara. "God, Jackson. What the hell have I done?"

"It was an accident. You'll be okay although you're going to be hurting for a while with a cast or boot on."

"Let us by, please." The paramedics brought a gurney and their equipment.

Jackson held her hand until they made him move, but he took up a spot near her head. "She's bleeding from the back of her head."

The paramedics checked her over, wrapped a bandage around her head, stabilized her ankle and moved her to the gurney. "We'll be taking her to Saint Luke's."

"I'll be there as soon as I can. I need to get a cab."

"I've already got a call into one, Jackson," Darryl said. "They'll be here in fifteen minutes."

"Thanks, Darryl."

"You can find her at the emergency room when you get there," the paramedic said as they moved her toward the ambulance.

"Jackson?"

"I'll be there shortly, baby. Hang in there."

"I love you," she shouted as they put her inside the ambulance.

"I love you too, honey."

He watched with a heavy heart as the ambulance drove away with her in the back.

The cab pulled up a few minutes later. When he wrenched open the door and hopped in the back, he told the driver where to go as he pulled out his cell phone to call her dad.

"Hey, Mr. Harris? This is Jackson Young."

"Hi, Jackson. What has Samantha done now?"

"She fell off the stage and it appears she's probably broken her ankle. I believe she has a concussion too, but we won't know anything for a bit. I'm on the way to the hospital to see what's up."

"Thanks for calling. Let me know when you know something about her condition."

"I certainly will, sir."

"Thank you for being there with her. You are a godsend, son."

"You're welcome. I love her so I wouldn't be anywhere else."

"That's nice to hear, Jackson. I hope she loves you too."

"She says she does, but after this I'm going to kick her ass. She's been drinking again."

"Oh man."

"Yeah, I could smell it on her breath after the fall."

"Lord have mercy."

"She's going to need it when I get done reaming her for this. She should have never been performing after she drank, but anyway, I'm at the hospital, so I'll call you after while."

"Thank you. Talk to you soon."

Jackson paid the cab driver and climbed out of the car. When he got his hands on his girl, he wouldn't be nice. This was way beyond something he would tolerate. She hadn't talked to him. He would bet good money, she didn't call Jacob either.

He stopped at the desk and asked for her room.

"She's being triaged in the emergency room. If you'll have a seat, the doctor will be out to get you soon."

Hadn't he just done this not two weeks ago with her? What the hell was she thinking?

He noticed a coffee pot sitting off to the side of the entrance. The liquid had probably gone stale, but it was better than nothing. He had a feeling tonight would be a long night.

# Chapter Fourteen

Jackson stood as the doctor came through the door and asked for whoever was with Samantha Harris.

"That would be me."

"Are you family?"

"Sort of. I'm her boyfriend."

"Well then, come with me. We'll talk on the way to her room."

"Thanks."

He led Jackson through the double doors as they headed down a long hall. "You are probably aware, she has a concussion and a broken ankle. We've stabilized the ankle, but she'll have to have surgery on it in the next day or two. It's shattered when she fell so she'll need plates and screws to hold it together. I've already consulted the orthopedic surgeon. He's planning on taking her to surgery tomorrow sometime depending on how her confusion is resolving."

"Confusion?"

"Yes. Typical of a concussion, she's repeating her questions and not sure where she is. She keeps asking for you, which is why you are coming back here so you can help calm her down. We don't want to give her any medication with her blood alcohol level." The doctor glanced at him, and then back down the hall. "Were you aware she'd been drinking?"

"Not until after she fell off the stage at the concert. She's an alcoholic and she's been recovering for the last week to ten days. Apparently, she started drinking again this evening before the concert."

"Her blood alcohol level is very high. Do you know what she drank?"

"My guess is whiskey. It's her drink of choice."

"She must have had half a bottle or so."

"She had a bout of blood alcohol poisoning about ten days ago, thus trying to get sober. Obviously, it didn't work too well."

"I'm sure you are aware it is a process and a long one for someone to recover from alcoholism."

"Yes, I know. My brother is her sponsor."

They reached a door to the right. "She's in here."

"Jackson!" She moaned. "Where's Jackson?"

"He'll be here in just a minute. The doctor went to get him."

"Don't be hard on her for now. The concussion wasn't severe, but it was enough to cause the confusion. Will you be staying with her tonight?"

"I will if they need me to. No problem."

"It would probably the best. The rooms upstairs have chairs that fold out into a cot. I've slept on them myself. They aren't too bad." The doctor held out his hand. "I hope you get her the help she needs."

"I hope so too."

"They'll be in to transfer her upstairs soon."

"Thanks, Doctor."

"You're welcome." He laid a hand on Jackson's shoulder before he turned and walked to the desk.

Jackson took a deep breath then pushed open the door.

"Jackson!"

"I'm right here, Samantha."

"Oh, thank God. Where have you been? I've been here for hours and they wouldn't tell me what's going on."

"You have a concussion and a broken ankle. You'll have to have surgery tomorrow to fix it."

She sat up higher on the gurney. "Surgery? Holy shit. I did a bang up job, huh?"

"Yeah, you did."

"What happened?"

"You tripped on something on the stage and fell off the front. You wacked your head and broke your ankle."

"Wow. I did a bang up job, huh?"

"Yes, you did."

"I'm repeating myself, aren't I?"

"Yes, but that's from your concussion."

"Sorry."

"They'll be transferring you upstairs before too long."

"How is everything at the venue?"

"I'm sure it's fine. The guys know their jobs. They'll take care of things. You'll probably have to cancel the next couple of shows until you're able to put some weight on your ankle or whatever they recommend. You might not be able to move around except on crutches for a while."

"This is going to put a real cramp in the show schedule. I had another one this week and one next week. The next six weeks were going to be very busy."

"I know, Sam. I know your schedule pretty well."

"Yeah, I guess you probably do."

Silence filled the room as she looked from him to the door and back like she was looking for an escape. That wouldn't happen with her injuries, but she definitely didn't want to look him in the eye for some reason.

A tear slid down her cheek. "I'm sorry," she whispered as her gaze came back to his. "I screwed up."

He didn't respond, figuring it was best for her to talk this out, but he did take her hand in his, rubbing his thumb over the knuckles to reassure her she could tell him anything.

"I couldn't stop, Jackson. I drank half a bottle before the show. I didn't do what I was supposed to. I didn't call Jacob when I had the urge to drink, I just downed that bottle like it was water."

"I know."

"You know?"

"I could smell it on your breath when I reached your side after you fell. The doctor also said your blood alcohol level is very high."

"I don't know what to do anymore."

"You need help."

"I know. I thought I was getting help and doing okay. I hadn't had a drink in ten days, but the minute things got crazy, I went right back to the whiskey." She grabbed the sheet lying over her to wipe the tears from her face. "What am I going to do, Jackson?"

He leaned back in the chair knowing he needed to be tough with her. This was important. "You need to talk to Jacob and to your doctor. Did you take your anxiety meds?"

"No. The bottle sounded better. I guess I should have taken it instead."

"Yeah."

"How was the show?"

"It was a good one. The crowd loved you."

"I don't remember it."

"That could be from the concussion or the alcohol."

She bit her lip for a moment before she said, "You know what's bad?"

"What?"

"I don't remember a lot of the shows I've done over the years."

"I'm not surprised."

"It's gotten better though. I guess my tolerance for the whiskey has cleared my memory some. Problem is, I just have to keep drinking more and more to get the same feeling."

"That's why they call it alcoholism, Sam."

"I'll try to do better. No more alcohol. I promise."

"You said that before."

"This time I mean it. I won't drink again. Ever."

"I hope you are willing to go that extra mile. You didn't seem to want to admit you really have a problem before."

She grasped his hand in hers, bringing it to her lips. "I do now, Jackson, honest I do. I know I have a drinking problem. I know I need help with it. You are here for me. I love you and I want us to be together for a long time to come."

"So do I."

"We'll be moving her upstairs now," the nurse said after she peeked through the doorway. "Give me a minute to get her paperwork together."

"Sure."

They made small talk for several minutes as they waited for the nurse to move her upstairs.

"I called your dad."

She blew out a heavy sigh. "Great. What did he say?"

"He's really worried about you."

"Did you tell him about the alcohol?"

"Yeah."

"Crap. I'll never hear the end of this now."

"You are lucky he's not flying out here to drag your ass back to Iowa and whup some sense into your head."

She laughed and he couldn't help but smile. "He would too."

"You're damned right he would. I'm tempted to take the situation under my own control and beat your ass myself."

"I might like it."

"You probably would."

The nurse came through the door, dropped her paperwork on the gurney and popped the break. "Are you coming up with us?" she asked him.

"Yes, ma'am."

"Follow me then."

Fifteen minutes later, they had her settled in a bed with her foot propped up on pillows as he sank down in the chair near the window.

"Are you staying the night with me?"

"I might as well. It's either here or on your bus and the doctor was worried about your confusion with the concussion."

"I think I'm better now though. I can remember some things but not others, and I'm not repeating myself."

"True, but it might be better for me to stay."

She glanced around the room. "I'd love for you to climb in this bed with me. I really don't think the nurses would like it much."

"No, the doctor said these chairs fold out into a bed. As long as they give me a pillow, I can crash here. I'm used to sleeping in much worse spots."

"I can imagine so."

He flipped on the television before asking her if there was anything particular she wanted to watch.

"No, not really. I'm kind of sleepy from the pain meds they gave me, so why don't you find something. I think I'll just get some shuteye."

"Okay. You let me know if you need anything during the night. They'll probably be waking you up regularly during the night anyway."

"Probably." She turned toward him. "Can you kiss me before I go to sleep?"

"Of course, darlin'." He got to his feet and walked toward the side of the bed. She really was cute with her hair in a braid down her back, her stage makeup was kind of smeared under her eyes, and her lipstick messy, but he loved her anyway. He leaned in and pressed his lips over hers. "I love you."

"I love you too, Jackson. Don't ever forget that okay? I know I'm kind of a mess, but you  mean everything to me."

Her eyes drifted shut before he even had a chance to reply. It was going to be a long haul with this drinking thing. If she was really willing to stop, he would stand by her.

* * * *

Samantha woke in the night confused as to where she was. The dark room frightened her in her state of mind until she turned her head to realize Jackson snored softly on the chair across the room. She knew he would never let anything bad happen to her.

Memories flooded back. Falling off the stage. Drinking before the concert even though she knew she shouldn't. It all came rushing in, bringing tears to her eyes. The call of the alcohol couldn't be shut off as easily as she'd thought when she talked to Jacob and her doctor at the ranch.

A choking sob rocked her body as she wrapped her arms around herself trying to hold everything in as her world came apart. If she lost Jackson because of this, she wouldn't be able to go on.

"Are you in pain, darlin'?"

"No."

"What can I do to help you?"

"Hold me."

He scooted up on the side of the bed as she moved over to make room. When he wrapped her in his arms, the world righted itself again instead of careening out of control. She knew he would always do this for her. She just had to figure out how to keep him around forever to be able to right everything for her.

"Better?"

"Yeah. Thank you."

"Anytime, honey. You know that, I hope."

"What am I going to do, Jackson?"

"What do you mean?"

"I'm afraid. I'm terrified, really, that I can't sing in front of the crowd without the alcohol in me. I'm not strong enough to overcome that."

He kissed the top of her head before snuggling her in closer. "Yes you are, Samantha. You have a beautiful voice. You are a very talented lady. You have to find some way to get past your fear. Maybe talking to a therapist would help."

"I have to do something or my career is over."

"You are a strong lady. You can overcome this. No problem."

"But what if I can't? What if my life as a country singer is over because I can't get up in front of people and sing anymore?"

He tipped her chin up with his finger. "You can handle this."

"What happens to us?"

"What do you mean?"

"What if I can't handle this? What happens to us?"

"Samantha, I'm not with you because you're a country star and have a bunch of money or whatever. I'm with you because I love you. Yes, at first I was in awe of you being Samantha Harris and that you were attracted enough to me to want to have sex with me, but it's not what made me love you. You are what made me love you. The way you are with everyone, the way you take care of people and everything. That's what's important. If your career was over tomorrow, it wouldn't change the way I feel about you. I will always love you, no matter what happens." He brushed his lips over hers, sweeping his tongue along the seam to encourage her to open for him.

This is what she needed—him. "I want you to make love to me."

"I can't. Not here." He kissed her forehead. "Besides, honey, your ankle is going to make things difficult for a bit. You're going to be in a lot of pain."

"I don't hurt right now."

"You have quite a bit of pain killer in you." He moved to the chair sitting beside the bed. "You need to sleep. You are having surgery tomorrow, remember?"

"Yeah. I hate being without food or water. My mouth is so dry."

"I'm sure having your blood alcohol coming down is doing that. I can see if you can wet your mouth, but you can't swallow any of the water." He climbed to his feet. "Let me ask the nurse."

"I'll hit the call button."

"Okay."

After the nurse came in and gave her some swabs to wet her mouth with, she settled back on the bed and closed her eyes. She needed to sleep so this whole ordeal would be over soon. The disappointment in Jackson's eyes hurt. It was a look she never wanted to see again, and by George, she would make it happen one way or another.

The next morning, they got her ready for surgery while Jackson waited in the chair in her room. She knew he would be there when she awoke, but she was still scared. She didn't like the feelings of coming out of anesthesia any more than she liked being hung over from drinking too much. It didn't happen often, but once in a while, she overdid and she would feel like shit the next morning.

She gingerly transferred herself to the gurney by scooting over as the nurse and the attendant managed her immobilized ankle. They had given her pain medicine earlier in the morning to numb it when they did this and she knew they would take care of her after surgery, but for now, she was too hyped up on adrenaline to care. "You'll be here when I get back?"

"Of course, darlin'. I'm not going anywhere."

"Thank you."

"For what?"

"For being here for me."

"I wouldn't be anywhere else. I love you."

"I love you too." The nurse tucked the blanket around her hips. "I'll see you in a bit."

"Yes, ma'am." He grinned before leaning down to kiss her. "You'll do fine, darlin'."

They wheeled her out and down the hall. She shivered under the blanket, from nerves mostly, she supposed, but the thought of going into a deep sleep terrified her.

"Are you all right? You look pretty pale," the nurse asked.

"I'm scared is all."

"It'll be okay. We have one of the best orthopedic doctors on staff. He'll get you fixed up and back on the road to recovery. You'll probably have to be in a boot for about six weeks depending on the damage, but he'll come talk to you and your boyfriend after all is said and done to give you the information you need."

"Thanks."

"Would you like another blanket?"

"That would be great."

She stopped the gurney next to a door. "Let me grab a warm one. Those are always fabulous when you are shivering like you are."

"Sweet."

After she had the warm blanket over her, she closed her eyes and relaxed on the gurney for the short trip to the operating room. She didn't remember much after that since they quickly moved her to the operating table, and put her to sleep.

She woke up several hours later, back in her own room with Jackson sitting at the side of her bed.

"Easy, darlin'. Are you in pain?"

"A little," she croaked. "Is it over?"

"Yes. A long time ago. It's seven-thirty in the evening now. You had surgery at ten this morning."

"Wow. I've slept all day?"

"Yep. I guess you needed the rest. I don't think you slept well last night. You moaned a lot in your sleep."

"I'm sorry."

"For what?" he asked, grasping her hand in his to rub his thumb over her knuckles.

"For being such a pain in the ass."

"I want to be a pain in your ass soon, but we have to wait a while."

"Oh, sounds like fun." She shifted on the bed. "I can't wait." Her body was on high alert from lack of sex. She knew this and she was sure Jackson knew it too, poor guy. Not that it had been a particularly long time since they had made love, but two healthy, active thirty year olds needed a raucous sex life, right?

"You need to heal first."

"Party pooper."

He pushed the button to call the nurse. "We can talk about the details of your surgery in a minute. First you need to eat something and probably get something for pain before it gets out of control."

"Good idea. I'm starving."

The nurse came in to see what they needed. "I'll get you a tray from the kitchen and be back in a jiff with some pain meds."

"Thank you."

The nurse gave Jackson a sexy little smile. "My pleasure."

After she left, Samantha sighed.

"What's wrong, darlin'?"

"Do they all have to flirt with you with me sitting right here?"

"She wasn't flirting."

"Yes, she was. Didn't you see that little smile she gave you? She wasn't looking at me like that."

"I don't know what you want me to do, babe. I can't help them talking to me."

"I'll use it to my advantage. You can ask them for stuff. They'll give it to you before they give it to me."

He laughed and shook his head. "Whatever you say, babe."

After she got some food and pain meds, she settled in to talk to him about the surgery and what would be required for her ankle to heal properly.

"The doctor said you'll be on crutches for a few weeks with a cast, but you might be able to graduate to a boot so you can walk around with it. Either way, you'll be in something for six to eight weeks."

"Great," she grumbled. "What about sex?"

"What about it?"

"When can we have it again?"

"I didn't ask."

"You didn't? Why the hell not?"

"I figured when you aren't in pain and we can maneuver your ankle so it doesn't hurt during, we would be good to go." He kissed her briefly, certainly not long enough for her taste. "Besides, you can ask him when you do a follow-up appointment with him in a couple of weeks."

"We can't stay here for two weeks. I have shows to do."

"Honey, I've already talked to your manager. We've cancelled the shows coming up for the next two weeks."

"You can't do that!"

"The hell I can't. Your health comes first and Billy agreed with me when I talked to him. We will reschedule when you are better. Your fans will understand."

She crossed her arms over her chest and glared at him. "Don't you ever get in the middle of my career again."

# Chapter Fifteen

"Excuse me?" The tone of her voice pissed him off. He was doing the best for her and her career and she was going to get pissy about him stepping in to rearrange her schedule?

"You will not get in the middle of me and my career. I will do the rearranging if things need to be rearranged. I will talk with my manager. I will talk with my record label execs. You will not."

"Now listen, Samantha. I did what was best for you while you were unconscious. I didn't think it was a big deal."

"It is a big deal. I will handle my career. I don't need you getting in the middle of it."

"If we're in a relationship, that means I'm in the middle of it. Get off your high horse and take a chill pill. We are in this together."

"You know nothing about my music career. You work on a ranch riding horses, herding cattle, and taking care of guests for a living. I've had to run this business on my own since I started. I know what I'm doing, you don't."

"What the fuck is your problem?"

"What's yours? Why are you trying to take over my career?"

"I'm not!" He threw up his hands as he began pacing from the window back to her bed. "I'm trying to help you, damn it! All I did was agree with Billy when he said you should cancel the next two weeks shows until you can get on the damn stage. You won't be able to climb stairs safely until you are in a boot. Stop being stubborn!" *What the hell?* He jerked off his hat, raked his fingers through his hair, and then shoved it back low on his forehead. "Listen, Samantha. I'm not trying to run this for you. You're right. I don't know the first thing about running a music career and I'm not trying to learn on a shoestring. I love you. I'm trying to be there for you and help you, not run things for you."

She glared for a full minute, he figured, before she lowered her gaze from his. "I'm sorry," she whispered. "You're right. I'm glad you cancelled the shows."

"I don't frickin' believe you. You jump my shit about making any kind of decision for you, and now you think you can make this all better by apologizing sweetly?"

"I can't?"

Frustration zipped through him. He rolled his neck a little to relieve the tension building there so he wasn't tempted to strangle her. "I need to take a walk." He headed for the door. "I'll be back." He slammed out before heading for the elevator. Coffee, soda, or something. He wasn't sure what he needed, but he would head to the cafeteria and take a break from her. Just for a few minutes anyway. The short ride down in the elevator did nothing to assuage his anger. He couldn't believe how she'd ripped him a new asshole about cancelling her shows and then turned on the charm to calm him down. How manipulative could someone get? Did she do that shit all the time with her producers, managers, agents, and so forth? He would have to watch her behavior a little more closely.

Oh, who was he kidding? He loved her. She could bat her eyelashes at him and he would be kissing her damned painted toes inside of seconds. Still, he needed to get away from her for a few minutes to calm down. She could still get his blood pressure up with her attitude some times.

As the doors slid open, he stepped out into the hallway, following the smells of food. His stomach grumbled. He probably needed to eat a sandwich or something since he hadn't eaten for quite a while. Breakfast, actually, come to think of it. He found the end of the line to the food, grabbed a sandwich, a Coke, and a small cup of some vegetable soup before he paid for his meal, and then went to find a table.

While he ate, he watched the crowds. Families with small children, men looking worn out, women with tears in their eyes, they all looked sad and forlorn making him wonder what their stories were. Obviously, they had family members here going through some kind of medical necessity, but his mind often ran with a scenario for each one building something out of nothing but a look on their faces.

He chuckled to himself as he finished his food. *I wonder if this is what Mesa goes through when she's thinking of new stories to write. Maybe I should sit down and chitchat with her sometime.* His mind always seemed to whirl with ideas about people he'd seen or talked to while he made up some kind of life for them out of his own thoughts.

He did see a gentleman with a large bouquet of flowers rushing through the lobby. Maybe a man with a new baby? Wouldn't that be fun, he decided. Sure, someday he wanted kids.

He frowned a moment when he thought about Samantha. Did she want kids? What kind of life would they have if she was on the road all the time? Where would they live if she was back and forth to Nashville all the time? These were things they needed to work out, he supposed, if they were to build a life together.

A life together. Was he really thinking along marriage lines? Yeah, he loved her, but did he really want to commit to a lifetime with her? A smile spread across his face. Yes, he did. He wanted to marry her.

With a gleeful lightness to his heart, he tossed his trash into the receptacle as he headed back to Samantha's room. He wouldn't ask her to marry him just yet. Something special would be in order for that moment, something he needed to think on for a bit. Besides, he needed to ask her dad for his permission anyway, which might be a little sticky since they really hadn't known each other all that long. He would have to buy a ring, something simple, but elegant like her. She always came across to him as someone who appreciated the smaller things in life rather than the fancy cars, big house, and servants kind of thing. Growing up a small town Iowa girl made her a lot like him.

When he approached her door, he drew in a deep breath hoping things had calmed down. He felt better for having taken the break, but they really needed to talk about her attitude. Now was probably not a good time. He pushed through the door to find the room dark. *She must have gone to sleep.*

He moved toward the chair in the corner and unfolded it into a bed so he could lie down and rest. Sleep would probably come hard tonight since he had so much whirling through his brain.

"Jackson?"

"Yeah?"

"I really am sorry."

"I know, darlin'."

"Are you still mad at me?"

"We'll talk tomorrow, but no, I'm not still mad."

"Good." Silence reigned for a minute. "I love you."

"I love you too. Now, go to sleep. We have to get you checked out of here tomorrow and back on the bus before we find somewhere to wait out the next two weeks."

* * * *

Two weeks. Two fucking weeks they'd been on the bus sitting in a small campground while the other band members went home for an unscheduled break. The other bus and rigs were parked at a storage place until she got the all clear for a boot so she could walk on her foot.

She hadn't been out of this can since she left the hospital and she was about to go out of her mind. Her appointment with the doctor was tomorrow, thank goodness, because if she didn't get out of here soon, she would kill someone, namely Jackson.

For a person who's normal routine included being outside on horseback working with his hands, he was surprisingly content to be on the bus tapping away at the laptop most of the time. She had no idea what he did all day while she rested and healed, but she'd had enough. If she didn't get a break soon, she'd go bat-shit crazy.

Jackson sat at the table tapping away at the keyboard beneath his fingers. The sounds grated on her nerves like nails on a chalkboard. Normally, it didn't bother her, but since she'd heard nothing else for two weeks, she was totally over it. "Can you please stop whatever it is you're doing?"

"I'm chatting."

"With who?"

"Jonathan."

"Jonathan?"

"My brother at the ranch. I'm asking how things are going and all that. I haven't really talked to any of them since your accident."

"Oh."

"Are you hurting?"

"No."

"Are you sure you don't need a pain pill? It's been quite a while since you've had one."

"No! I don't need a pain pill. I need to get the fuck out of this bus before I go stir crazy."

He turned in his chair to look at her. His eyes sparkled with mirth.

She wanted to throw something at him.

"Please, Jackson. I need out of here. I need to breathe some fresh air, go outside, go to the store, go to a movie, something. I'm about to go crazy."

"We can watch a movie."

"At a theatre?"

"I guess. I can carry you inside, put you in the seat and then carry you back out. We would need to call a cab since moving the bus is a silly idea."

She sat up straighter in her chair. Writing songs had become a chore like everything else since she'd been hurt so that wouldn't help matters, but getting out of here would. Anything to see outside again. "I can walk on my crutches as long as you are spotting me."

"Okay." He turned back toward the laptop. "Let's find a theatre around here and we'll go see something."

She bounced in her chair excitedly. "Thank you!"

After he managed to find somewhere they could go to see a movie, he helped her pull on a coat. She couldn't make it off the bus without him carrying her because of the width of the stairs. Of course, she didn't mind being in his arms and if she managed to lick his neck, bite his ear, and generally make him horny in the process. Well. Her job was complete.

"You'll pay for teasing me later, you know. I'm going to drive you insane before I let you come."

"Promises, promises."

"Definitely a promise," he said as he helped her maneuver into the cab. "After all, I let you pick the movie so that's another reason to torture you later since you are making me watch a chick flick."

"I need a good cry."

"Why?"

She wrapped her hand around his bicep and leaned into his side. "Because being cooped up has pissed me off. You're lucky you still have a head, but since you were nice enough to take me out, you'll live to see another day."

"Hopefully, the doctor will put you in a boot tomorrow and you can get around again, do your shows, and be a normal human being." He kissed her on the nose. "You should have been writing songs the last two weeks, but you haven't been."

"I didn't feel like it. I've been too grumpy to write."

"Too keyed up?"

"That too although the sex has helped a lot."

"I'm glad I could be of service to you, milady."

"Aw, aren't you such a handsome devil. I think I'll keep you around for a bit."

"So nice of you to say so. Besides, you can't get rid of me that easy."

"I hope not. I like having you here."

"I like being here."

"Good."

They pulled up to the theatre a minute later. He paid the driver before he got out and went around to her side of the cab. She scooted her butt around on the seat when he opened the door, then slid her cast out to rest on the ground before he helped her put the crutches under her arms. They managed to get inside without too much trouble, pay for their tickets and then hobble her inside the specific room where the show they would be seeing played.

"Do you want me to get popcorn and Coke?"

"Of course. What is a movie without popcorn?"

"I'll be right back then."

While he was gone, she let her mind wander to Jackson. She really did love him more than she could ever show him. He'd been there for her, helped her in every way, and supported her like no other had ever done in her life. Yes, she loved him with all her heart. She hoped he loved her as much. They would work out the details of where they would live soon, she hoped. She had a lot of ideas she wanted to bounce off him.

He returned several minutes later with a huge tub of popcorn and the biggest cup of something cold she'd see in a long time.

She wet her lips thinking about the Coke in that glass. What she wouldn't give to put a little whiskey in with it right now. This being clean and sober sucked pretty badly when all she wanted was a little alcohol to take the edge off. She would feel so much better if she had some, but it wasn't to be, at least for now. Darryl wasn't around to get it for her at the moment.

"You okay?"

"Yeah, why?"

"You're quiet."

"You're supposed to be quiet in a theatre."

"Not until the movie starts."

"I suppose."

"Are you thinking about getting back to singing?"

"A little. I'm nervous about it."

"You shouldn't be. I've told you before, you are very talented and you've got a great show."

She tilted her head to the side. "You aren't just saying that because you love me, are you?"

He leaned in and kissed her on the lips. "No."

"Okay." She reached over to grab a handful of popcorn. "Thanks."

The movie made her cry, big, blubbery girlie sobs she couldn't hold in if she tried. She needed the cry though. She'd had so much pent up frustration, anger, and just general bullshit tied up inside her, she had to let go somehow. Now, she could move on.

They waited for the crowd to disburse after the movie before she hobbled out on her crutches to the lobby.

"I'll call the cab company. We might have to wait a few minutes though."

"No problem." She sipped the last of the Coke, making the contents gurgle in the bottom of the cup. "We can sit here and chill until they get here."

A young woman about seventeen shyly walked up to them. "Are you Samantha Harris the country music singer?"

"Yes I am. Do you like country music?"

The girl gushed. "Oh yeah. You are my absolute favorite singer. Can I get a picture and an autograph?"

"Sure, doll."

She should have known. The moment it got around the movie theatre she was there, she had a line of people wanting autographs and pictures. This she didn't mind. She actually loved being with her fans, talking, taking pictures, and all of the stuff that went with being a popular singer even though most days she didn't feel like it.

Jackson asked the cab company to come back in thirty minutes so she could take care of her fans.

God, she loved him.

She sighed and closed her eyes for a moment. "Tired?"

"Yeah."

"Want me to cut this off?"

"Yeah, I think so."

"Folks, I'm sorry but as you can see Samantha hurt herself a few weeks ago and tonight is the first time she's been out since the accident. She's really tired and needs to go rest. She'll be doing another show in the area in the next couple of months, so please make sure you check it out, get tickets, and come by. She would love to see you."

He grabbed her crutches, scooped her up in his arms, much to the sighs of some of the ladies in the crowd, and carried her out to the cab.

The ride back to the bus was made in silence as she rested her head on his shoulder.

Tomorrow would be a busy day. She hoped the doctor would put her in a boot and she could start performing again. Her stomach knotted. She needed to get over this before the next show.

When they reached the bus, he helped her out so she could hobble to the stairwell before he swept her up in his arms again to carry her inside. *Such a gentleman.* "Are we going to make love now?"

"If you want to. You seem really tired. I figured we could wait."

"I am tired, but not too tired for you."

He let her hobble into the back bedroom before she sank down on the end of their bed. Everything in the bus belonged to him too, these days. He'd certainly made himself at home when he moved into her space to live. His shaving cream and toothbrush took up space in the bathroom, his underwear and socks had their own drawers in her dresser, his jeans hung in the closet along with his western shirts. Yep, he'd moved in and taken over her life. She didn't mind at all.

She slipped off the T-shirt she'd worn to the movies, tossing it to the pile in the corner of dirty clothes. Her bra came next, leaving her completely bare to his gaze. His eyes sparkled with lust as his gaze slid over her. "Do you want me?" she asked, her voice barely coming out in a whisper.

"Hell yeah, I want you."

"Take me then." She laid back on the bed so he could help her take her pants off over her cast. They'd been really creative with the sex since her accident, but tonight she didn't want creative, she wanted down and dirty, hot and sweaty sex. "Fuck me."

"I'd plan to torture for a while, but I don't think I can wait. I want you too bad." He quickly stripped off his clothes. "Can you turn over?"

"Yeah." She flipped on to her stomach, then shuffled back so her butt was on the edge of the bed. "What's your pleasure, cowboy? Back or front?"

"I want your hot little pussy first, then I'm going to take your ass."

She shivered. Lord, she loved making love with him and to have him take her this way was the best. His cock bumped at her opening, the piercing sliding enticingly along her vaginal walls as he slowly pushed inside her. "Holy fuck."

"You are so tight."

"I love how you feel inside me. Go hard."

He slammed his pelvis against her butt, as they both moaned. The quick thrust of his hips brought her to the brink of an explosive orgasm within minutes as he pounded into her from behind. She loved hot, dirty sex and Jackson was the master of it from the experiences she'd had with him. His hand went around to between her legs and he rubbed her clit with a rapid you-will-come-now rhythm. She exploded in an earth-shattering climax as lights danced behind her closed eyelids. "Oh God."

He panted behind her. She could almost feel him gritting his teeth to hold back his own climax. "You okay for me to go up the back?"

"Hell yeah."

"Okay." He pulled his cock from her pussy, smearing cum along with it up the crack of her ass. She was so hot and slick, they wouldn't need any lube this time. "Deep breath, sweetheart."

He pushed his dick slowly through the puckered hole at her ass, past the ring of muscles and stopped until she felt her whole body relax with his penetration. "Oh yeah. Perfect."

His hips began the slow thrusting motion meant to keep his own climax at the surface, but not allow him to fall over, she knew from experience, but it would bring her to another climax shortly if she knew her own body very well at all. She felt her pussy throb with each beat of her racing heart. Sweat slicked her skin. Goosebumps rose from the cooler air hitting her. She needed this more than he knew.

"Please, Jackson. Harder. Faster."

"I want this to last."

"I'm there, baby. I swear. Fuck me."

He growled low in his throat as his thrusts became uncoordinated, hurried and rough. Her body shattered on a high-scream climax she knew would stay with her for a long time to come.

# Chapter Sixteen

Apprehension slid down her back. This was the first show since the accident. Jackson was out doing his rounds before the show began. She knew she wouldn't see him until after the whole thing was over.

Her stomach knotted.

She'd already taken two Xanax to calm her nerves. It hadn't done anything. She took three more just a few minutes ago.

A knock sounded on the door.

"Come in."

Darryl climbed the stairs a minute later, the brown package in his hands, her lifesaver.

"Are you sure you want to do this, Samantha?"

"I have to, Darryl."

He handed her the paper bag. She blew out a breath as she opened the bottle and took a long swig of the whiskey. She could feel her body relax that quickly. Her life is what it is. She couldn't do this without the whiskey, she just couldn't.

"I'll leave you to it then. You're on in thirty."

"Thanks, Darryl. You are very important to me, you know."

"I'm your supplier, Sam. I don't like it."

"But—"

"Nothing. Jackson is going to kill me, but I can't say no to you." He walked out without a backward glance.

For the next thirty minutes, she drank. Big swigs, little sips, it didn't matter, she needed the alcohol.

She sat back against the cushion of the couch as she let the alcohol take effect. Her eyelids felt heavy. Maybe a little nap would be a good idea, but didn't she need to be somewhere? She couldn't remember. Oh well, Jackson would take care of her. The couch cushion looked so soft. She would just close her eyes for a few minutes and then she would feel a lot better.

* * * *

Jackson knocked on the door of the bus. Samantha was supposed to have been on stage five minutes ago and he hadn't seen hide nor hair of her. *She must be messing with her makeup or something.* He got no answer.

He opened the door and bound up the stairs, worry rushing through him. It wasn't like Samantha to not answer the door.

Holy fuck!

He rushed to her side when he spotted the three quarter empty bottle of whiskey on the table along with her bottle of medication for anxiety. "Samantha?" He shook her shoulder. She didn't even moan. He peeled back her eyelids. Her pupils were pinpoint. "Samantha?" She started to throw up so he rolled her on her side and held her there as he screamed for some help. Darryl came rushing up the steps.

"What's going on?"

"Call an ambulance. Now!"

Darryl's hand shook as he dialed 911.

Jackson prayed and prayed hard. *God, please let her be okay so I can beat her ever lovin' ass for this.*

"Samantha?" He rolled her onto her back, pushing her hair out of her face. "God, Sam, please, don't die."

"She's going to die?" Tears ran down Darryl's face.

"No, damn it! She's not going to die, but you need to get yourself together. Go out and tell Mark what is going on so he can direct the ambulance. The band needs to cancel the show. We will reschedule it for another time, but for now, get these people out of here."

"Okay."

"Darryl?"

"Yeah?"

"Do you know where she got the booze?"

"I gave it to her." The smaller man shook from head to toe. "I'm sorry, Jackson. She asked me to get it for her and I did. I know she drinks too much, but I figure she'd only drink a little so she could get on the stage, not like this."

"You do realize this is bad. I don't know what the hell is going on here, but it's bad."

"I know. God, I'm sorry."

"You should be, now go do what I told you."

Darryl practically ran down the stairs and out the door. Mark came in a minute later. Jackson gave him a run down. "I don't know if she took some of her medication or not with the alcohol. Right now, she's breathing but very shallow. This could kill her."

"The ambulance should be here in a minute."

"Okay. Get them up here immediately. I'll carry her down to them so they can work on her."

"All right."

He held her hand watching her chest rise and fall. *Keep breathing, baby, keep breathing.*

The ambulance arrived as he scooped her up in his arms and rushed down the steps to their waiting gurney. "All I know is she probably drank three quarters of a bottle of whiskey and possibly took some Xanax. They are prescribed, although she's not supposed to have the alcohol. She's vomited as you can tell by her shirt. She won't respond to her name." He raked his fingers through his hair, not even sure where his hat ended up. "God, help her, guys, please."

As the paramedics went to work on her, getting her vital signs and putting a needle in her arm, he paced. *She has to be okay. She just has to be.*

They decided to put a tube down her throat to make sure she didn't breathe in any vomit and to help her respiration since it was so shallow.

"We are taking her to Mission Hospital. Will you be following?"

"I'll be right behind you."

Someone called a cab while all hell had broken loose, thank goodness. He didn't know what he would do without the group he had around him. They were great people and cared about Samantha a lot. Unfortunately, they'd been through something similar with her twice now so they knew what to do. He would let them handle the show, breaking it down and getting everyone situated.

He followed the ambulance to the hospital praying the whole time. He didn't know what else to do in this case. No one close to him had ever been in this situation before. He wasn't sure how to handle it other than doing what he'd done when she had alcohol poisoning. He would talk to the doctors and go from there.

This hospital shit was for the birds. He'd done it way too often with her in the short time they'd known each other now, but by God damn, he'd had enough with her. She was going to find some inpatient rehab or something because he couldn't keep going on like this.

He found a cup of coffee after he let the receptionist know who he was there with and began to pace. He needed to call her dad...again, and he really could use a shoulder right now. Maybe he'd call his mom or no, Jacob. Jacob would know how to handle this.

Grabbing his cell phone, he pulled up his brother's number and hit talk.

"Jackson, what's wrong. You never call me."

"It's Sam."

"What happened?"

"I'm not sure other than I think she drank most of a bottle of whiskey. I think she took some Xanax, too, but I don't know for sure until I talk to the doctor."

"Do you think she was trying to commit suicide?"

"Hell no! Why would you say that?"

"The combination of those two could kill her."

"I know that, Jacob, but I don't think suicide was what she was going for. This was her first show after her accident. You know how terrified she is about getting up there. I think she couldn't handle it without the alcohol. Darryl got it for her. He's been supplying her apparently."

"He needs to find a new job."

"Yeah, I know."

"Who is here with Samantha Harris?" the nurse called as she came out the doors.

He raised his hand as he walked toward her. "Me. Listen, I need to go, Jacob, prayers would be good."

"No problem, brother. Call me later."

"Okay."

He followed the nurse through the doors and down the hall to a curtained off area to the right. The doctor was at Samantha's bedside. "Are you with her?"

"I'm her boyfriend, yes."

"Do you know what happened tonight?"

"From what I saw, she must have drunk three quarters of a fifth of whiskey. There was also a bottle of Xanax on her table near where I found her."

"That doesn't surprise me. We found benzodiazepines in her system when we did the toxicology screening. Her blood alcohol is very high. I'm glad the paramedics intubated her. She's not out of the woods yet, but she's stable. We will be transferring her to the Intensive Care Unit until we can take the tube out of her mouth, which may be a couple of days. It's going to take at least twelve hours for her to come around." The man's face got serious. "You don't think she was trying to commit suicide, do you?"

"No, sir. I talked to her earlier. She was fine. She's never had a problem with depression or anything like that, but she does have an alcohol problem we've been working on. Not very successfully from what it appears."

"What's up with the boot?"

"She broke her ankle falling off the stage three weeks ago after another bout with the alcohol."

"Sounds like you've got your hands full."

"Yes, sir, I do."

"The nurse will let you know when they are ready to transfer her. You won't be able to stay with her in the ICU, but there is a family waiting room outside you can stay in unless you are going home."

"Home is her bus at the moment, sir."

"I see. Is she some kind of performer?"

"Yes. She was supposed to do a show at the amphitheater tonight. She's a popular country music artist."

"Okay. Well, I will leave you to sit with her. You can talk to her if you like. We don't know how much a person who is sedated or in a coma can hear, but it doesn't hurt to talk,"

"Thank you."

"You're welcome. I hope you can help her. She seems to have some rough stuff going on."

"Very true."

Jackson took a seat next to her bed. He picked up her limp hand in his, wrapping his fingers around hers in a grip he knew would probably bother her if she was awake. He needed something to hold onto. She was completely out of control and he wasn't sure he was strong enough to help her anymore. Inpatient rehab would be something he would have to bring up when she got over this. She wouldn't like it, he knew, but what else could he suggest? Doing it on her own obviously wasn't working.

He listened to the sounds of the machine breathing for her. It scared him. All of this scared him out of his mind. "Honey, I hope you can hear me. I'm right here for you. I know you didn't do this on purpose, baby, but we have to talk about this as if you did something you knew would hurt you. God, what am I going to do with you, Samantha? You can't keep doing this to yourself. I know you're terrified to get on that stage. It is just something you're going to have to get over some other way than with alcohol and drugs."

A tear slid down his cheek.

"I don't think I'm strong enough to help you through this. I thought I was, but I don't think so anymore. You need someone to be there who is a professional, someone who knows how to deal with this kind of addiction.

*What the hell am I going to do?*

He didn't say anymore to her even after she woke up and they took the tube out of her mouth. He couldn't bring himself to talk rehab to her until she was strong enough to answer some questions for him. The answers from her would tell him how to proceed.

"Can I go home today?" she asked, three days after she'd arrive at the hospital.

"Yes. The doctors will be in to release you this morning."

She looked like hell. Dark circles rimmed her eyes, her skin was pale and translucent, and her demeanor seemed timid at best. This wasn't the woman he'd grown to love. She was a shadow of the girl he knew.

He didn't know what to say to her anymore so their conversations were strained.

When they finally made it back to her bus a few hours later, he decided it was time for them to get this out in the open so he could make some decisions about their lives…his life.

* * * *

Samantha struggled up the steps on the bus. She just wanted to get back to normal with Jackson. The last three days had been hell on both of them and she wasn't sure how to fix it. They needed to talk, she knew that, but where to begin.

After she got settled on the couch, she leaned back, propped her booted foot on the coffee table and got comfortable. This was going to be a long talk.

"Talk to me, Jackson. I can't stand these stilted conversations between us. We haven't really talked in three days. Hell, you haven't even kissed me since I woke up for being intubated."

"I know. We need to talk, but I'm not sure where to start."

"From the beginning?"

He threw up his hands before they settle back at his sides balled into fists. "God damn it, Sam. You could have died!"

At least he was talking to her. Not that she liked the way this was starting, but it had to start somewhere. "I know, Jackson. I'm sorry. I don't know what you want me to say."

He tossed his hat on the couch before raking his fingers through his hair. "You don't have a clue, do you?"

Deep in her heart, she didn't know what to do, what to say to fix this. He meant everything to her. "I guess I don't. Tell me what to do. I'll do anything to make this better."

"I can't, baby. If you don't know, I can't help you. You have to want help."

"Help me, Jackson."

"You don't even know what you are asking for help with."

"No, I don't, but if it is something you understand that I don't, make me understand. Help me understand what it is that is so shattered inside of me."

"That's just it. You don't know." He paced from one side of the small enclosure to the other with his hands fisted at his sides like he was trying desperately not to reach for her.

She wanted him to hold her, touch her, make love to her, but if he did, it wouldn't mend the broken fences. His grey eyes looked sad as he fought with some demon she couldn't fathom. If he'd only tell her, she would do anything for him.

"I'm done, Sam."

"Done?"

He stopped pacing, facing her with hurt and anger in his gaze. "I can't do this anymore."

"Please, Jackson, don't say that. I need you."

"No. You need the alcohol and the pills, you don't need me."

"Is that what this is all about? I'll quit. I can do it. No problem. I don't need them, really I don't."

"I've heard those words several times, Sam, but you keep going back to them every time things get stressful. We've had this conversation. You said you'd stop the drinking. You didn't, you just hid it from me. When it came down to it, the habit put you in the hospital and almost killed you. I can't sit back and watch you destroy yourself, I won't."

"I love you. Please." She held out her hands, hoping he'd take them like he'd done so many times before in the last several weeks. She needed him. She couldn't do this without him. Tears clouded her vision.

He didn't budge. He grabbed his hat from the couch, placing it on his head before adjusting it to sit low on his forehead. "I'm sorry, Sam."

Her cowboy. He was walking out on her.

He slowly turned, walked to the three steps that lead out of her door, never looking back once.

The door popped into place as she slid to her knees in the middle of the floor of her bus. The tears were coming in streams now, running down her cheeks as sobs wracked her body. Her body shook from the emotions running through her. *What the hell am I going to do now?*

* * * *

Jackson called a cab to head for the airport. He hadn't even packed his shit. It didn't matter. He was going home, back to Thunder Ridge. Until Samantha Harris figured out how to beat this problem, he couldn't be with her. She had to do it on her own or had to figure out how to get the help she so desperately needed to beat this addiction.

Lucky for him, a flight would be leaving in two hours for San Antonio. He'd already texted Jacob to meet him at the airport so his ride was in place to be home in his own bed within a few hours. The flight home wouldn't take long.

By the time his butt hit the seat, he leaned back, closed his eyes and tried to relax. He hadn't slept much the last three days with Samantha in the hospital.

It was going to be difficult explaining everything to his family.

He turned his head and looked out the window as the lights of California faded into the night sky. The roar of the engine lulled him a little. Really, he had too much on his mind to be able to sleep anyway.

The tears in Samantha's eyes almost broke his resolve. He had to stay strong. His thought on the matter was if she loved him enough, she would get the help she needed. He hoped it worked because he didn't know what else to do. Tough love. If it didn't work, he would have to learn to live without her for the rest of his life.

As he stepped out of the baggage claim area to find Jacob, he sighed wondering what Sam was doing now. She'd probably flipped out after he left. What if she went on a drinking binge again and there was no one there to call an ambulance? What if she died this time? How would he ever forgive himself?

*Maybe I should call her.*

"No. She needs to figure this out and being strong for her is the only way. Besides, Mark is with her. He'll take her wherever she needs to go and hopefully, that's home."

When he saw Jacob's truck, he opened the door and slid inside.

"Hey."

"Hey."

They pulled out into traffic headed for the airport's exit. The signs flew by as he stared out the window, lost in his own thoughts.

"You okay?"

"No. I just left the woman I love to struggle through this on her own, Jacob. Did I do the right thing?"

"Man, I wish I knew. I hope she calls me, but I don't know if she will. She needs help, Jackson, professional help."

"I know."

"So what exactly happened the last few days?"

After he relayed the entire story to Jacob, his brother whistled softly.

"Wow."

"Yeah."

"So what's the plan?"

"I'm home. That's it."

"Nothing else?"

"I'm hoping the tough love thing will work and she'll seek out some professional help as in inpatient rehab. She needs it for like a few months."

"I agree."

The rest of the ride was made in silence as he lost himself in the terrible feeling he had in the pit of his stomach. If he didn't do the right thing, he could have just pushed her right over the edge into something he didn't want to acknowledge. She might actually try suicide.

# Chapter Seventeen

Three damned months. He hadn't heard hide nor hair about her in three damned months. He'd talked to her manager, but got nothing but vague answers from Billy. He got more info from the media, which said she cancelled all her shows indefinitely without really saying why.

His life had become a living hell without her. He couldn't sleep, couldn't eat, couldn't work without messing shit up, and he certainly couldn't fuck another woman.

A month after her incident, Darryl had been arrested for stalking. Apparently, the young man went to her bus after he'd left, confessed his love for Samantha and professed his adoration would find no end if she would just love him in return.

The mission had worked. The stalker had been revealed and her supplier was now in jail so hopefully she would get the help she needed.

*Where is she? What is going on with her and why haven't I heard anything? Nothing new in the media, nothing from her parents, nothing from her, her manager won't talk to me and the guys in the band are silent as well. This shit sucks!*

He walked out of the barn headed for the main lodge. He wanted to talk to his mother to find out what he should do because this living without Samantha wasn't working.

A black sedan caught his attention as he walked past the cabins, up the gravel area, and past the old hitching posts stationed strategically throughout the property.

*Nice car.* It wasn't really his type, but the shiny black exterior was definitely sharp in the early spring afternoon.

He took the steps two at a time to reach the big wooden door to the inside of the lodge. The dining room was quiet this time of day as lunch had been served an hour or so ago and supper wouldn't be out for several hours. The guests usually took this time to go for afternoon rides, play horseshoes, go swimming or just hang out around the ranch.

When he made his way through the large living space, he thought he heard Samantha's voice coming from the back of the room. He shook his head. She couldn't be here. Imagining her showing up to tell him everything would be okay, that she'd spent the last three months in rehab getting clean, wouldn't lend him any favors.

He rounded the corner of the table and came to a stop. Someone was in his mom's office.

The woman turned at the noise he made with his boots on the floor.

It was Samantha.

She climbed to her feet before turning toward him. "Hi."

"Hey."

"I was talking with your mom a little before I came to find you."

"I see that."

"Can we talk somewhere private?"

"My cabin is free."

"Sounds good." She turned toward Nina. "Thank you for your advice. I appreciate it and I'm sure everything will work out like it should."

"You're welcome, Samantha. Let me know if you need anything else."

"I will."

She followed him out and across the yard to his place. Nerves racked his body. What was she doing here? Where the hell had she been? She seemed sober, but then again, she didn't always drink during the day. She had the problem with it before shows.

After he opened the door and waved her in, he shut it behind them as she took a seat on one of the chairs near the window.

"How have you been?" he asked as he sat in the chair across from her.

"Fine."

Silence. God, he hated the silence, but he needed to let her tell him why she was here.

"Uh, I've missed you."

"I've missed you too."

She sighed and looked down at her hands. "I guess I should start with what I've been doing the last three months since you left."

"That would be good."

"I cancelled all my shows."

"I heard that much."

"I found a great rehab facility in Nashville. I've been there drying out. I haven't had a drink since the incident at the concert with the alcohol and the Xanax." She sat forward in her chair. "I need you to know something, Jackson. I never intended to hurt myself. I took the Xanax to calm down for the show. I forgotten I'd taken some, so I guess I took more based on what the labs results showed in my system. There was way more there than the one or two pills should have been. Darryl brought me the whiskey. I downed half the bottle. I couldn't face going out there without it."

"You've been in rehab?"

"Yes. I've been sober for three months. I feel really good. I'm seeing a therapist and I think I've got my shit together now."

"That's great."

"I don't know if you can forgive me or not, but I had to tell you what's been going on. I don't expect you to want back in my life after everything you've been through with me. I needed you to know something. I love you. That hasn't changed one bit since you walked out, which by the way, thank you. Knowing you weren't going to put up with my drinking anymore kicked me in the ass. I needed the smack upside my head."

"I'm glad I could help."

"If you don't want me in your life, I understand."

He dropped to his knees in front of her, taking her hands in his. "I love you, Samantha. That hasn't changed. I've been miserable without you, but I knew you had to do this on your own. You needed to make the decision to get help, otherwise, it would never work. I'm glad you've been sober for three months. I hope it continues."

"It will. I'm done with the alcohol. I've even been writing some and singing. I've done a couple of shows, small ones, but shows nonetheless where I haven't needed the booze to bolster my self-esteem. They've been fabulous and I've even made some new friends in the recording business. Some of the artists who've had problems too, have come forward to help me get my confidence back to sing again. I've also found out all of the animosity I felt from them was self-perceived. They did like me, but they thought I was aloof and hard to approach so they kept their distance."

"That's fantastic."

"So do you think we can start over and be boyfriend and girlfriend again?"

"I'd like to very much."

"Me too."

He put both of his hands on her face, bringing her closer so he could kiss her. God, he missed her more than anything in this world, and he wasn't going to let her go again, not in this lifetime.

# Epilogue

Christmas found them gathered around the huge tree in the main lodge of the family's guest ranch. They had been splitting their time with her touring, recording, and doing the fan stuff with spending time on the ranch with his family.

Life had been almost boring without the frequent trips to the emergency rooms in various states where they traveled.

Her career had taken off again after she came clean with the media about her drinking problem. She had a new CD coming out in the next month and her new single was already climbing the charts.

"Where are you two headed next?" Nina asked from her seat on the couch as the grandkids ran around the lodge.

"Back east. I have a couple of shows in the south and two up in the northeast." Samantha took a bite of sugar cookie. "These are fantastic."

"Wow. This time of year is bad for travel," James added.

"Yeah, but her bus driver is one of the best and so are the rig drivers. They can handle it."

"When is the new CD coming out?" Mesa asked.

"Next month, but don't you dare go buy it."

"Why is that?"

"You'll have two then, but I'm not saying anything else."

Jackson stood near the mantle with his arm resting on the wood as he drank his Coke. They never had alcohol in their home anymore, not even for him, which was fine. He didn't need it anyway. She'd been doing great so far and he didn't want to give her any reason to backslide. He would protect her with his life.

Tonight was special. They hadn't really talked marriage yet, but he was ready. The ring was burning a hole in his pocket as they sat around making small talk with his family. He just needed the right moment.

Everyone settled down and quiet descended on the group.

*Now would be great.*

"Samantha, can you come up here with me for a minute."

"Sure, babe."

She got to her feet and weaved her way through the kids on the floor as they waited for the grandparents to say it was time to open presents.

"I wanted to do this with my family present and on such a great holiday as Christmas." He got down on one knee as he took her hand in his and pulled out the marque cut diamond solitaire. "Will you marry me?"

Tears rolled down her cheeks as she whispered a soft, "Yes."

He got to his feet and wrapped her in a warm hug before kissing her on the lips.

"Ew!"

They laughed as they separated.

"When's the wedding?"

"Oh my! I have a wedding to plan now."

"Don't worry. We are all old pros at it. We'll help," Mesa volunteered as she held her eight month old little boy on her lap. "Right ladies?"

Peyton, Paige, Callie, Candace, Terri, and Nina all agreed.

"I would love for all of you to help. I've never done this before so I'm kind of lost."

"No worries. We've got you covered," Paige said as she grabbed Hannah when she ran by.

The entire group shouted at the same time, "Welcome to the family!"

# *The End*

# About the Author

Sandy Sullivan is a romance author, who, when not writing, spends her time with her husband Shaun on their farm in middle Tennessee. She loves to ride her horses, play with their dogs and relax on the porch, enjoying the rolling hills of her home south of Nashville. Country music is a passion of hers and she loves to listen to it while she writes.

She is an avid reader of romance novels and enjoys reading Nora Roberts, Jude Deveraux and Susan Wiggs. Finding new authors and delving into something different helps feed the need for literature. A registered nurse by education, she loves to help people and spread the enjoyment of romance to those around her with her novels. She loves cowboys so you'll find many of her novels have sexy men in tight jeans and cowboy boots.

www.romancestorytime.com

# Other books by Sandy

Love Me Once, Love Me Twice (Montana
Cowboys 1)
Before the Night is Over (Montana Cowboys 2)
Two for the Price of One (Montana Cowboys 3)
Difficult Choices (Montana Cowboys 4)
Doctor Me Up (Montana Cowboys 5)
Stakin' His Claim
Country Minded Cougar
Meet Me in the Barn
Taming the Cougar
The Call of Duty Anthology
Five Hearts Anthology
Trouble With a Cowboy
Gotta Love a Cowboy
Make Mine a Cowboy (Cowboy Dreamin' 1)
Healing a Cowboy's Heart (Cowboy Dreamin' 2)
For the Love of a Cowboy (Cowboy Dreamin' 3)
Tempted by the Cowboy (Cowboy Dreamin' 4)
Forever Kind of Cowboy (Cowboy Dreamin' 5)
Kiss Me, Cowboy (Cowboy Dreamin' 6)

# Secret Cravings Publishing
## www.secretcravingspublishing.com